To Ana.

THE TRANSLATOR'S BRIDE

I

My return trip is gloomy, rain falls relentlessly and I stick a hand out of the window, the streetcar moves slowly, someone crosses the rails in a hurry, there's shouting and swearing, these people are so wearisome, I bring a hand to my face, get it wet in a disgusting fashion, the woman in front of me turns her head away, there's nothing else she can do, my face is damp, maybe it's obscene to wet one's face in front of a lady one doesn't know from Adam, I'm ignorant of such issues, the streetcar heads off again, outside a woman carrying multiple net-bags lifts a broken umbrella in the air and rants, she would surely like the streetcar driver to take responsibility for the damaged umbrella, he might as well pay her the repair, she screams and shouts so much I can still hear her as we move forward, she's right, of course, it wasn't her fault, and if we consider that the accident wasn't an accident, we'd have to hold the streetcar driver responsible, that fool didn't brake on time, the good-for-nothing, a pervert, if it were him selling the tickets he'd steal from the blind without flinching, the scoundrel won't admit the damage he has caused.

Nevertheless, the streetcar heads off, truth be told the scoundrel can drive, rain isn't letting up, I feel sad, going to the pier didn't comfort me, that weight in my stomach got worse, the little woman in front of me has a very tempting tiny little nose, I feel an urge to nibble it, yes, it's a radish, how I would like to bite it, hear it crack under my teeth, how charming, marvelous, would she mind me having a go?, would she, or maybe not, my mouth is drenched in saliva, I've always had this problem, I produce too much saliva, she turns her head away once more, she's a lady, in profile her tiny nose is still a lovely radish, but, for God's sake, this is outrageous, no doubt, what am I doing leaning forward, almost touching her knees, my mouth open, what an idiot, a real jerk! Ladies of this kind shouldn't be approached so rudely, open-mouthed, saliva pouring down one's chin, what a sorry sight, the nerve one must have to present oneself like that to a lady, this sort of woman shouldn't be on a streetcar in the first place, no, they should only be transported in calèches drawn by the finest horses, or even in one of the ever-increasing number of vehicles that circulate in the city, and whose exhaust pipes release a nauseating smoke that smothers the sweet smell of equine dung, if deprived of these reminiscent odors, how will I be able to remember the months spent at my grandma's home, given the fast pace of progress they will indeed become impossible recollections in a near future, and well, these fine ladies are in their domain when seated in those motor vehicles, the chauffeurs speeding over the curbs to take them to the theater, the opera, they hold the door open for them and display chivalry like professionals, a genuine finesse, these ladies walk with delicate steps, they climb the theater stairway under showers of praise, words of encouragement, they shouldn't have to lean on other passengers, wobbling from one side to the other, enduring such a torment, the little woman's bag opens, heads of garlic scatter over the streetcar floor, a toothless fidgety boy laughs, he's not the slightest bit ashamed of his mouth, a little prick who laughs when he sees the heads of garlic rolling on the floor, the woman tries to catch them, she can't avoid smelling the reek of sweat coming from the passengers in the aisle seats when she comes closer, it's preposterous, an opprobrium, the things we see on public transport are simply repulsive, nobody bothers to get down and help the woman pick up the heads of garlic, I would do it myself were it not for the risk of being misinterpreted, I've had my share already with the open mouth drenched in saliva, what would the passengers think if I bent forward to help her, finding myself face to face with her, perhaps biting her radish nose, how mortifying, no question about it, I would help her anyway, if that didn't taint her honor in front of these brutes, the little arsehole is still laughing, he's got one of those faces that generates a desire for violence, I'd smack it all over, what an idiot, I bet he wipes snot under his school chair, a disgusting pig, no, I can't help this lady, society doesn't understand selfless solicitude and I feel too despondent to do it, I've been shattered since I returned from the harbor, where I saw her depart.

The ship set sail and she didn't say goodbye, she didn't utter a word, she didn't even make a gesture, must have forgotten to do it, it's only natural, it's perfectly normal, one doesn't go on a trip like this every day, it's difficult to embark in these conditions, in this weather, yes, there's nothing odd about it, how could she raise her hand and wave at me when the wind was such that she could hardly hold her umbrella climbing up the steps, followed by so many hasty passengers who couldn't be bothered with goodbyes, yes, how? But why am I thinking about these details when there's nothing I can do about it now, cannot even help the woman pick up the heads of garlic, she still hasn't managed to pick them all up, goddamn it, this is too much, is she shortsighted or plain clumsy? Or, even worse, is she trying to perpetuate this unbearable situation, just to fumble about and touch the passengers' feet? What a debauchery, this streetcar is full of animals, it's grotesque, that kid can't close his toothless mouth, he keeps laughing like an idiot, and this woman crawls on the floor, chasing heads of garlic that she never picks up, good Heavens, how did I find myself in this den of bestiality, and God only knows who else is in here, I should ring the bell immediately, get out and explain the situation to the streetcar driver, but how could I do it when he is himself a rogue of the worst kind, a vile destroyer of umbrellas, of course, how could I expect to find myself among civilized people if the driver is an ass, what an awful situation, painful!, I don't want to turn my head and see what surrounds me, I'm afraid of what I might see, were it not for this heavy rain I'd get out immediately, the walk would do me good, it would help me forget that sorrowful farewell, if she'd at least waved at me, smiled, thrown me a kiss after touching her lips with her fingers, then I'd feel happier, wouldn't have to contemplate this sad spectacle, this freak show.

However, I can't resist, I might regret it but I'm compelled to turn my neck, it is probably an unwise decision, I'm not sure if I still control my own body, someone in this streetcar could be playing with my mind, I don't believe in fairy tales, nonetheless certain unfathomable phenomena occur too many times to be seen as mere coincidences, there are indeed extraordinary occurrences, ghosts, sudden feelings of sickness, spells, ailments of various natures, God knows whence they come, the fact is that I turn my head, the damned lad is still openmouthed, I wonder why he's laughing so much, if he's laughing at me and not at the woman who, on all fours, searches for the heads of garlic, her bag opens up a little more and I can already see an onion rolling with the movement of the streetcar, there're a lot of passengers, the vehicle's not running at its fullest, but there aren't many seats left and then why, Lord, why do I have to turn my face . . . there she is, an old lady with a huge wart, disgusting, she's got a very noticeable moustache too, she must've just arrived from a village, this is no longer in fashion here, how sad she doesn't have a daughter who could talk to her about how disgraceful she looks, the old woman smiles, seems about to open her mouth and laugh out loud, maybe it's the imbecile kid's fault, that despicable little redhead whose mother doesn't teach him any manners, she's sitting dead silent next to him, please madam, tell him to close that mouth, that gutter, I avoid looking the old woman in the eye, she might want to start a conversation with me, I don't feel up to it, I'm a wreck, finished, devastated, what will my life be like from now on, she departed in that ship without a return date, said she didn't want to see me again, we'll see if that's how it's going to be, she's displeased, life isn't easy, I admit it, I must think, meditate, but first I need to get off this streetcar, the journey is endless, it takes longer in this rotten weather, the rain doesn't stop, I force myself to turn my face to the window, some drops fall on my shoulder, I brush them off, they've gathered there for a long time, I got distracted, the damned woman can't pick up the heads of garlic, now she's running after the onion, I feel an urge to shout disjointed words, insults, can hardly restrain myself, the passengers are barely speaking, that's unusual, it isn't normally like this, perhaps the rain descends upon them as a melancholic veil, it's funny how water and fire can have such similar effects, though they nullify each other, the fascination we feel when we're close to a bonfire is not that different from the sweet sensation conveyed by rain hurled against a window under an opaque gray sky, a fire-red sunset isn't too bad either, I feel the need to stretch my hand and catch the falling rain drops, needles that shatter my skin into minuscule pores, so little that I can't see them, I wish I could open my mouth and swallow the rain, my head stuck out of the window, turned toward the clouds, give me something to drink, this abundant saliva dries a man up inside, what a nuisance, the streetcar is at a standstill, there's a wagon full of flowers on the rails, the mule refuses to walk, it's afraid, these damned tin cans, the automobiles, fill the air with exhaust, the mule can't see or think in the midst of so much smoke, the mule's owner hits it but to no avail, the streetcar driver, that scoundrel, rings the bell and rants, he's gotten soaked over the course of his route and is insufferable, people come on and get off but he stays there, always standing while he cranks, breaks, and accelerates; the vehicle doesn't move forward, at last the heads of garlic come to a halt, the respectable lady and her radish nose manage to pick up most of them, only one keeps escaping, it ends up sliding to the feet of the toothless lad with the idiot grin, the obnoxious kid feels it touching his foot and kicks it, a rascal, another scoundrel, maybe he's related to the driver and didn't even pay for his ticket, his mother says nothing to him, the old woman with the wart opens up a bit more her hairy smile, certainly addressed to him, the respectable lady sees the head of garlic fly in my direction, this is preposterous, here I am with all my problems and yet have to witness this scene, determined to take a stand, I bend forward and pick up the head of garlic, get back into my original position, and offer it to the lady with my open hand, poor thing, she doesn't deserve this, she smiles and returns to her seat with her bag full again, she thanks me with a nod while she accepts the head of garlic that I triumphantly proffer, the kid isn't laughing so much now, bloody idiot, if I caught him in a dark alley you'd see in what state I would leave that stupid ginger, they wouldn't recognize him at home, maybe the old woman is scratching her wart, I hear the distinctive sound of a nail scratching skin but can't bring myself to turn my neck and see for myself, I suddenly get up, the driver is still gesticulating at the flower seller, the mule won't move, I gesture to the respectable lady in front of me, I understand her agony, we live surrounded by depravity, perhaps my damp face isn't as intolerable, as obscene as before, I almost step on her toes when I get up, bump my head on one of the overhead handles and quickly move forward, don't look back, walk past the driver and he stops talking for a while, the villain wants to impress me, he thinks I'm an important man, it's truly repulsive to see what lowlifes these people are, the mud where these swine wallow, well, he won't get anything from me, an absolute zero, I go forward, the jerk tries to tell me something but I walk past him, couldn't care less if I shouldn't get off here, can't stay inside any longer, it will be faster if I walk, the rain doesn't bother me, I jump off the streetcar, feeling a bit of moisture on my face is actually soothing, she left without so much as a wave!, I walk away from the streetcar, the mule seems tired of standing there and gets on moving, the flower seller runs after the wagon, the streetcar can now move on, the bell rings, how funny!, I feel my hair getting drenched, water runs over my eyes yet there's no wind, so the whole picture is rather bizarre, what rain is this, the streetcar follows the tracks, the beasts are all still inside, the rain hurts my eyes, I don't need to lift my gaze from the sidewalk, but, for some reason I cannot fathom, that's precisely what I do, some inexplicable circumstance disturbs my mind, it could be her departure, or some other random thing, something supernatural, witchcraft of the worst kind, the truth is that I look at the streetcar and see the respectable lady who was sitting in front of me waving a hat through the window, what could she possibly want, she opens her mouth and utters something, I can't make out what she says, her words are muffled by the racket produced by the wet rails.

Water runs down my face, I raise a hand to my head, that's right, I entirely forgot about my hat, had placed it on the seat next to mine, the respectable lady must have noticed it after the streetcar headed off, it's too far now, I'm not going to run after it, how embarrassing, my God, how embarrassing, it's pouring and I still have such a long way to go, without a hat or an umbrella, a miserable pauper, a beggar, Helena has gone and left me here, alone, damp, how shameful, what will those animals on the streetcar think, the kid must be laughing riotously, the old woman with the wart does the same, a merry group indeed, how mortifying to get off without remembering my hat, nonetheless everything could be fine, it would have been an honorable exit, yes, had I at least not picked up that head of garlic!

II

I take the key from my pocket, my hand is cold from being so wet, I insert the key in the lock, the door to the building is stuck again, my coat is soaked, damn door, the landlady won't get this fixed, I'm compelled to use all my strength, almost force the lock open, passersby gaze at me, I look like a burglar, I'm not even wearing a hat, nothing but a wretched man standing in the merciless rain, the gathering clouds wish to make rivers overflow, at last I manage to open the door and enter the hall.

Darkness has taken over this house, Mrs. Lucrécia saves on expenses, not even a measly candle is lit, how can one live in such conditions, that miser disconnected the electricity, claims what she receives from her tenants doesn't allow for such a luxury, I work by candlelight in the winter, strain my eyes in my obscure and musty little room, there's no respect for a man's work, oh no, translation is not a profession a reputable person would have, after all, why on earth would someone pay me to scribble a few sentences on a page, to render business letters, invoices, first-class literary works into our noble language, forget about that my good man, grab a hoe instead, become a doctor in the medical arts, then you wouldn't have to sleep in this sordid room rented from Mrs. Lucrécia, a widow who sucks her poor tenants dry, and speaking of the devil, there she is, coming down the stairs, the crone looks like an elephant, a rhinoceros, those fat paws make the whole floor tremble, she's a hippopotamus, a genuine ungulate beast, what an ugly mug!, she hasn't reached the bottom of the stairs yet and is already gasping for air, a human kettle ready to explode, what she saves in light bulbs is more than enough to fill that paunch, all day long my room is invaded by the odors of cooking, I'm only entitled to three thrifty meals but this huge batrachian braises, roasts, and fries from morning till evening, when she passes by us we get a whiff of the stench of fries, I'm not allowed to smoke indoors, the smoke bothered her, she couldn't enjoy the smell of her stews, the flabby carcass has just come down the stairs and before I can greet her a word comes to my mind, damn, I forgot what language it is and what it means, *kartofler*, yes, but how terrible, what a mental obscenity, right when I have Mrs. Lucrécia before me.

"Morning, morning! I haven't seen you yet today. You didn't come down to the dining room for breakfast. I was worried about you. In fact, I was so worried I've just gone to your room, to see if you were all right. I didn't see you leave."

The greedy harpy winks at me, or at least that's how I interpret that sinister facial contraction, the shadows don't let me make it out clearly, she's holding a candle in her hand but her body absorbs most of the light, it's grotesque, the rain beats against the windows and slides down, I feel the cold inside the building bite my body under my damp clothes, I need to go upstairs, she left less than an hour ago and I'm already in this pitiful state, I have to pull myself together.

"Mrs. Lucrécia, you didn't have to! An engagement forced me to leave earlier, much to my sorrow. You know how much I enjoy your lovely company at breakfast. It always makes me feel bright and gives me strength to face the day. All that due to your wonderful smile!"

Mrs. Lucrécia smiles, her eyes are slits of darkness in the midst of the rosy swellings covering her face, she comes closer, what a hot breath coming out of those lungs, it's a complete aberration, how can nature tolerate the existence of such a being, it contradicts all evolution, with this woman humanity goes back centuries, thousands of years, she's certainly not aware of the newest scientific theories, she's not the reading type, I have brought her magazines with articles I have translated, but the ass insists on saying she doesn't have time to read about mundane matters, she'd rather inhabit the ether of her kitchen, a parallel, strange universe, the damn word doesn't seem to get out of my head, I almost feel like saying it, have to restrain myself from doing so.

"You're always so chivalrous! What could an old woman like me possibly have to offer to such a cheerful man?"

Nothing, of course, but I have to work.

"A lot, Mrs. Lucrécia, you have no idea how much you are needed in this world, disaster spreads like plague, a war ends just so others can begin, we are governed by shameless, corrupt, egocentric politicians, the people are uneducated, our youth are lost, they don't appreciate the traditional values and religion of our blessed society, yes, as you can see, you are a beam of light that illuminates us in this putrid air, a self-sacrificing, altruistic soul, you do good regardless of when or to whom you do it. By the way, Mrs. Lucrécia, could you spare me a little candle, please?"

The old woman smiles at me, I can't get the word out of my head, *kartofler*, damn it all, why can't I think of Helena right now, instead of being upset by so many stupid, useless things, for crying out loud, this is torture, I was born at the wrong time, otherwise I could have been a figure from Greek mythology, a god fallen into disgrace, the savior of mankind, condemned to eternally suffer while facing the absurd, a gigantic rock that I roll and carry on my back, everything inside me wants to explode, I shiver with cold, water trickles down my neck, I left my hat on the streetcar, God knows where it is now, will have to look into that.

"But of course, I'd do anything to please my tenants! Oh, this isn't exactly a business, it's more like family, and nobody is treated better than those I welcome under my roof."

A bright soul, Mrs. Lucrécia, she undoubtedly treats us like family, she welcomes the wretched poor under her roof, so long as they pay her in due time, you can't ask much more than that, that's true, the old woman steps back a little and opens a drawer with one of the keys on the bunch tied to her large waist, she's got dozens of candles there.

"Do try and make it last, please, they're worth their weight in gold, and it's already the second I have given you this week."

"I know, Mrs. Lucrécia, but I must work, a man has to earn a living!"

"Yes, that profession of yours is truly unpleasant, it wears you out. Have you ever considered finding a new job, one that gets you out of the house, working in an office all day, or in a shop? Your boss would then pay your wages . . . and for the candles."

"Who knows, Mrs. Lucrécia, maybe one day I'll do it, I have thought about it, but this is the only thing I can do, really . . . I am rather feeble, I suffer intensely with my bronchitis, but maybe in the spring, after the rains . . ."

Mrs. Lucrécia smiles in approval, I step away slowly as I speak, got already one foot on the first step when she throws me a couple of breathless words.

"Today's lunch will be delicious. I've already started cooking it."

"Thank you, Mrs. Lucrécia. Could you please tell me the time?"

"It's now half past eight, sharp."

"Thank you so much, Mrs. Lucrécia, you're an inexhaustible source of wisdom. Just one more thing . . ."

The old woman draws near, I lean over the banister, I'm standing on the second step, bent over, I've soaked the carpet, water is dripping from my body, I shiver with cold, can't help it, it's stronger than me, the fat widow stretches her neck, I come closer, can smell her breath of greasy Sunday roasts, she hasn't digested them yet, overnight wasn't enough, she anxiously waits, I shout into her ear.

"*Kartofler, kartofler, kartofler!*"

Mrs. Lucrécia looks at me perplexed, she doesn't know what to say, her ear is probably still reverberating, she suffered with my shout, what should I do, I can't control everything that happens in the world, my body is part of it, it's impossible to dominate it entirely, even partly, I'm relieved, feel much better, the bloody word wouldn't leave my mind, I don't remember what it means, nevertheless, releasing it very loudly seems to have helped, it broke whatever spell it had on me, I hesitate before the old woman's face, she's not speaking and neither am I, then I decide to hurry upstairs while talking over my shoulder.

"Thank you, Mrs. Lucrécia, God bless you! What a relief, believe me. See you at lunch."

I run up the stairs with the candle in hand, I don't look back, my landlady is perhaps still flabbergasted at the bottom of the stairway, every step groans under my frozen feet, I take the key out of my trousers pocket, my hand is still stone cold, can hardly move my fingers, I open the door, am back in my room, I'm shaking all over, there's no heating, just a bed, a chair, a closet, a desk covered with papers and books, a basin filled with water, I've had enough of water, there's not much light coming into the room, I close the door and throw the key and the candle onto the bed, it's so cold in here, this is what a man works for, one lives a wretched, sad life, has to deal with idiots all day long and there's not a single trace of warmth when he gets home, I start to undress, get a clean towel from the closet, and dry my body . . . good Heavens, it's so cold, I will never be warm again, I might die here, I can already feel the pneumonia, yes, it affects me, will boil with fever until I die, Mrs. Lucrécia won't call the doctor, she's afraid she'll have to pay him herself, no, I'm not leaving this room anymore, except in a coffin, I feel an urge to cough, the disease is galloping, fulminating, I stand stark naked, enveloped only by the towel, the rain falls more sparsely now, the sky appears to be clearing, yes, the sun is bursting through the clouds, it might not be the case if I were outside, the universe is plotting to kill me, I have no luck, misfortune haunts me, instead of having a star illuminating my birthday, I came into this world accompanied by a horn, a big, twisted, white ox horn, black at the tip, how ridiculous, don't know what I'm thinking, the word comes back, relief was only temporary, I wonder if she's feeling well, whether the sea is billowing, she's never traveled on a ship before, she has so many days of journeying ahead of her, my God, I'm going to die here, I have to get dressed, nobody is looking after my health, I'm on an empty stomach since yesterday's dinner, I didn't eat a thing while I was out, I feel weak, I put on dry clothes and rub my hair with the towel, get into bed, cover myself with the blankets, the light of a timid sun filters through the window.

III

I'm awakened by a smell of stew, the fragrance of peas creeps into the room through the door cracks, oh, not the stew again, I look through the window, there are fewer clouds in the sky, what time might it be, I haven't wound my watch, it's lying on the desk just like any other useless object, sunk in papers, I get up, I managed to warm up though I'm still freezing, maybe it's all this longing, taking into account the fuss outside it must be noon, the cashier girls walk out the shops for their lunch break, I have to go downstairs, I think of her, where might the ship be now, wish I had a huge map, the size of this room's wall, where I could mark the journey of the ship, she's heading north, a little dot on the blue section, next to the country that has been painted pink, or brown, or whatever color it is, nothing but a grain in the vastness containing everything I care about, why do I have such a sorrowful life, I burn everything around me, I'm hoarfrost, and all this thinking about her makes me want to feel something palpable, I open the closet and search for her scarf in the drawer, it still has her smell, hold it close to my nose, the scent of stewed peas fills my nostrils with the acrid tallow in which they marinate, the reddish gravy disgusts me, have to go downstairs, my stomach growls and demands food, I put the scarf back in the drawer, close it, sneeze, the pneumonia has already snared me with its claws, it must be the flu anyway, or a cold, the sneeze doesn't repeat, maybe I'd better put on a clean tie, Mrs. Lucrécia likes to see me looking prim and proper, and one never knows when I might need a new candle, all this is obscene, a cultural perversion, what am I doing here, Lord Almighty, why didn't I sell what little I had and buy a ticket too, if I were to sleep in an alley full of snow I wouldn't be worse off than here, the mold gets into my skin and makes me rot, I feel myself actually getting older by the second, the watch has stopped, I approach the desk.

Upon the enormous mess of scattered papers I see an envelope with my name on it, forgot about it, that's right, it arrived yesterday, it's from Valido, the book publisher, that leech, what could that stingy crook possibly want to summon me to his office for, I'm going to call on him this afternoon, I don't even have a hat to present myself properly, that's fine, will carry my old umbrella and he probably won't even notice, that rat's most likely blind to such things, he still lives in the last century, has a fat bank account, his passbook is as thick as the Bible, but he doesn't miss a chance to save some money, I bet he doesn't even eat lunch so that he can save a bit more, the miser should pay his employees better, he's so full of himself just because he published a handful of good books . . . oh well, what else can I do but to go, work is scarce, they owe me plenty but don't pay much, hell with all this, I feel like tearing up the letter, yet I know I will go.

What an abject life, my stomach growls louder and louder, it can probably be heard in the room next door, the student with the goatee might be sleeping, he said he was studying law, though I'm more inclined to think he studies the bottom of wine glasses, in itself a deep and serious field of study, a complex science, a comprehensive system involving repetition, eternal return, history within itself, a true wonder, the cup empties itself and is refilled, the student has been analyzing this process for the three years it's taken him to complete his first year of Law School, I have already told him he has to make up his mind, the rogue twisted his mouth and shrugged, he wears a monocle despite having perfect eyesight, he even bought a cane to uphold his finesse, as well as a bowler hat, and thus the smug scholar spends the money his father sends him, the foolish man remains in the village happy for a son who will one day become a lawyer, poor man, he may never see that day coming, *kartofler*, *kartofler*, *kartofler*, bloody hell, this is too much, unbearable, I let go of the tie and fumble with the papers, where's the damn word, I can hear Mrs. Lucrécia tapping on the tureen with the spoon, it's the last call, if I don't hurry I will eat nothing but pea skins, I toss the papers onto the desk, look at myself in the mirror above the basin full of freezing cold water, one could die here, this cracked mirror doesn't bring me good luck, curious things are happening in my life, I must ponder all that in more detail, someone will surely be able to inform me about good and bad fortune, the tie looks great for someone who is about to eat with a hippopotamus, a billy goat—only if he wakes up!—and a water rail, now this is a proper zoo, I shall have to charge an entrance fee, perhaps this way she can finally afford to pay the electricity bill, Mrs. Lucrécia sleeps with all her money stashed under her pillow, I was told such a gruesome fact by her maid, a poor slave who hardly ever leaves the kitchen, the old hag will get a hunchback with all that money piled up under her pillow, her neck will be deformed, she'll be a freak, on the other hand, I'm not sure if it's a zoo or a circus, the only attraction missing is the bearded lady, it's a shame the old woman with the wart doesn't live here, or we'd have a full troupe.

I look great for someone who has barely slept, these few hours in bed were a blessing, I dreamt about her, I open the door, then close it, the key always tucked away in my pocket, one can't trust these people, I go downstairs, the carpet has dried while I was sleeping, I head into the dining room, they're all there already, Mrs. Lucrécia is standing in front of the tureen, steam all around her, a Greek prophetess amid the sulfurous smoke exhaled by the earth, the student reclining on the chair, his goatee and hair in disarray, his dark eyes bloodshot, he's a billy goat, I seem to spot traces of vomit on his white shirt, what an utter disgrace to present himself like this in front of ladies, Miss Sancha is impeccable as always, she works in an office not far from here, says she has many suitors but spends every evening locked in her room, she must surely communicate with all these gentlemen by letter, which is fine, much more hygienic too, a girl as cold as she is barely needs the warmth of physical contact, no, it would destroy her, she's too fragile and appreciates relationships strictly confined to paper, as is fit to someone whose work implies reading lines of passbooks, she's now waiting to be served, the student wavers, I pull a chair and sit down.

"We thought you weren't coming. We were surprised you didn't show up for breakfast," Miss Sancha is also very kind when addressing someone. She's a rose, fresh as can be.

"Yes, indeed, a prior arrangement constrained me to be in a distant place at a time unsuitable to share a meal with such a refined young lady. I'm so very sorry, trust me. It pained me so much not to see your beautiful fingernails in the morning, Miss Sancha!"

"My, my, always so courteous," our beloved Miss Sancha is always considerate, no doubt about it, with her smile and pretty fingernails and all that. "You surely must have missed Mrs. Lucrécia's breakfast."

Of course, how couldn't I miss that rancid fat, I even looked forward to eating such a fabulous meal all night long . . . Mrs. Lucrécia looks askance at me while she fishes for peas in a sea of grease. No doubt she's already stuffed, she takes her time before filling my plate, my stomach growls embarrassingly, hopefully my companions will link such a noise to the reveler next to me. The paunchy crone must still be shocked at my indecent behavior, that mysterious word is now as upsetting to her as it is to me, conquering her dear affection seems to be the only solution left.

"But of course, of course! Who wouldn't miss the company of Mrs. Lucrécia, this precious lady! Look at you, Mrs. Lucrécia, you're a true Valkyrie!"

Mrs. Lucrécia turns her face, blushes, she thinks she's a Valkyrie, she even bats her eyelashes.

"Well, let's not exaggerate."

"Not at all, just look at you, ready to serve Odin, so ethereal, flying well above the wretched humans!"

"Hmm, your knowledge . . . I have no idea what you're on about."

"Modesty, Mrs. Lucrécia, is one of your strongest qualities."

And so is frugality, judging from what is floating on my plate, half a dozen peas in a disgusting broth, I think I saw a piece of carrot as well, but it might also be a fingernail, not from Miss Sancha, though, or a simple illusion, for my brain has been playing tricks on me; indeed, such abundance can hardly be real.

"Still, you put me on a pedestal."

"But of course, Mrs. Lucrécia, you're such a wonderful cook, such a selfless lady, gifted with a pure heart of solid gold, gold so solid you could bite it and break your teeth, yes, in this dining room I come upon a real mythological scene, a Valkyrie before me, a nymph at the head of the table—our dear Miss Sancha . . ."

"And how about me?" grunts, under a great strain, the student.

"You're a leprechaun. One of those useless leprechauns, a faun, or maybe a servant of Bacchus. Yes, you're a true bacchant."

"Then I'm a bacchant . . ." the student smiles idiotically, he is elated with the epithet of bacchant, the big dimwit, oh yes, he's the real deal, the greatest personality to come out from his neck of the woods, and his father pays for it . . . so much effort to pick up this rotten fruit . . . what a brute, what a brute.

"So, do you enjoy the stew? Would you like some rice?"

"Yes, yes, please."

Mrs. Lucrécia serves me the rice, a gooey mush which drops onto my plate like grout, the gravy spatters my tie, well done, I don't have another clean tie, the filthy hag doesn't notice anything, God, why do I have to live in this pigsty?, why? Luckily, some peas survived the attack.

The student sticks his head in the plate, slurps the gravy, while Miss Sancha, polished as always, raises the fork to her mouth, I'm not quite certain that she actually chews, my landlady eats with a spoon, she's foul mannered, it's a lack of respect, of dignity, and now how am I to present myself to Valido, that scoundrel lives as a badger but he's surely capable of noticing what I'm wearing, or isn't he?, can't quite remember what he's capable of, my tie is all greasy, my sweet Helena is at sea, I wonder if you can hear me?, a small dot on the blue, smoke coming out of the ship's funnels, I am surrounded by these imbeciles, so much coarseness, I must save enough money for the ticket and leave, she promised to send me a telegram once she arrived, this miserly Lucrécia doesn't even have a telephone at home, with what she gets from us she might as well have one, makes no effort at all to improve her tenants' conveniences, I must have a serious talk with her, maybe around spring, when the days are longer, won't need candles by then, I can even sit in the garden with my papers, as long as it's not windy, should I make it there alive, of course, I feel a mild tickle in my throat, maybe it's a cough, the cold attacks my respiratory system, I'll be very lucky if I don't get double pneumonia, damn streetcar driven by a scoundrel, that toothless boy is also to blame, forgot my hat, I wonder if I can get it back, on whose head is it now stuck, possibly full of lice, ticks, these people don't bathe, there is no hygiene, all I can smell are those traveling tin-cans invading the streets and a pestilent stench of urine, tar, and filth, this city is a dump, a den of rubbish, I hope foreigners drink enough so as not to notice this horrible odor, they can feel it as soon as they disembark from the ships, it's not a smell of sludge but of concentrated humanity, too many people, the rain washes it away to an extent, nonetheless there is an everlasting reek coming from basements, sewers, the plumbing, trash bins, the greatest stench comes from people, I swallow the rice and the peas, all flooded in gravy, this grease will satiate me for several hours, I'll feel comforted on this damp day.

"Ladies, please forgive me for devouring this meal in such unusual haste, but it's time for me to take my leave, and therefore I cannot enjoy your cheerful company any longer. I hope I will see you at dinner," and I stand up, the women wipe their mouths with napkins, the student looks as if he's about to say something, but he holds back and remains quiet. "Mrs. Valkyrie, Miss Nymph, Mr. Bacchant: I bid you farewell."

The women prattle with each other, they giggle like school girls, the bacchant growls, I move away from the table, reach the darkened stairway, the sky is very cloudy, I climb up two steps at a time with the intent of leaving as soon as possible, I open the bedroom door and rummage in the closet, search for my umbrella, stow the publisher's letter in my pocket, take a quick look in the mirror, put on my coat, which is still a little damp, there's no other coat to replace it, I empty my wet trousers pockets and transfer the contents to the ones I'm wearing now, close the door and go down the stairs, the next minute I'm outside, the umbrella under my arm, I decide to walk to the office, thus saving the streetcar fare, the sidewalks are wet, there are puddles everywhere, wagons mingle with automobiles, a little girl is selling oranges, I buy one out of compassion, her face is smudged, maybe it's deliberate, a trap, for Christ's sake, how hard can it be to wash a child's face, it is surely a scheme to lure morons like me, well, I've already bought the orange, it's not the little girl's fault, she smiles at me with her toothless mouth, I put the orange in my pocket, walk, and hang the umbrella on my belt, it's not raining, I feel a sudden urge to smoke, haven't smoked since yesterday, a man of few addictions, I reach into my right-hand pocket and take out a matchbox and a cigarette I had previously rolled, unfortunately it's a little wet, but there's no other, so this will have to do, I stop and protect the trembling match flame with one hand, winter is terrible for matches, what a dreadful thing it must be to be a match, to exist only to burn, I wonder if this moment is repeated countless times, if the universe expands and contracts to create itself once more, if a demiurge interferes and toys with atoms, this match may have burned hundreds of times, I've gotten my feet wet hundreds of times too, what a ridiculous life it would be, no, I sincerely hope to die and remain buried, nothing here will be missed, my only joy is Helena, her dark eyes and dark hair, her fair skin blushes when shyness surprises her in her modesty, the dimple that appears on her left cheek when she smiles, her features are now aboard a ship, how many miles must it have traveled already, perhaps there will be more departures in the future, I wish there wouldn't be, the cigarette dries at last, I've already used three matches, now I manage to light it, I put the matchbox back in my pocket, lift my head and exhale the smoke through my nose, the umbrella is still hanging from my belt, I'm ridiculous, a penguin, I'm not wanted anywhere, not even in the zoo, some people pass by slowly, maybe they deserved a little show, some somersaults and other acrobatic deeds, no doubt they'd love to see me executing all those exuberant tricks, flipping and turning in midair, however, I turn my face and see a yellow house with a small front garden, a camellia, rosebushes, a lemon tree laden with fruit, the small house looks cozy, it has a low chimney that resembles a stool, I would like to sit up there, over the entrance an iron and glass structure protects the vestibule from the rain, its small windows are rimmed with green-painted wood, the same color as the gate and iron fence, this is all very graceful, it reminds me of something, yes, I remember passing by this same house with Helena, we stopped on this very spot during one of our walks and she was delighted with the little house, she smiled, I asked her if she liked it, she said she would love to live here, spoke with sadness, we can't afford it, perhaps she was already thinking about leaving, I had no idea, but if this house was mine we could get married, she would return and never feel like leaving again, this house could be the solution, why didn't I think of this before, who dwells here?, I see a fat cat at the window, it probably belongs to an old lady blessed by luck, what does an old woman need this for, one must give way to the young, isn't the creature aware of this?, so many wars, deaths, illnesses, plagues of various natures, crises, political coups, insurrections, prices always rising, it's revolting, it should be mandatory to let go of properties like this one after a certain age, well, it's possible that the old woman or whoever lives here is considering selling the house, I shall come round later, I need to go to the weasel's office now, if the secretaries go out to run errands he won't open the door, he's too important a character to welcome visitors himself, always busy, he takes note of all his expenses in his greasy little notebooks, each candle is scrupulously noted, inkwells, priceless pieces of jewelry, I take the umbrella from my belt and stare one last time at the house, it's lovely, no doubt about that, delightful, a woman becomes even more elegant in a little house such as this one, might paint it pink, it would look nice, Helena with her coat and scarf in front of the recently painted façade, a cat at the window, the roses blooming, I can plant an almond tree, can tell there's a backyard, this house is my salvation, the solution, I'm so sorry I didn't think of this sooner, it's an excellent idea, will ring the doorbell when I return, but now I must proceed.

IV

The streets are all muddy, this neighborhood is a swamp, the ideal lair for a weasel like Valido, I walk the last few yards with extreme caution and the support of my umbrella, I'm afraid I might slip, not even mules could walk here, I feel a momentary doubt, have to check if I brought the letter with me, there's something in every pocket, in one of them an orange, in another the keys, here's the letter, moist and limp, I'm holding it in my hand when I knock on the door, I wait a few moments and knock again, after a short time a woman answers it.

"Good afternoon, madam," I touch my forehead, trying to lift the hat I'm not wearing.

"Good afternoon. What can I do for you?"

"Yesterday I received a letter from Mr. Valido summoning me to his lofty facilities on this pleasant street. Here it is, should you wish to confirm it."

"Yes, of course, please come in."

I come in, she closes the door, it's very dark inside, only one candle lit on a desk, the light almost concealed by the heap of documents piled up to the ceiling, I don't see anyone else in the room, there are closed doors leading elsewhere, I notice the smell of burned tar, something strange is going on, I seem to even sense a slight odor of sulfur, maybe it's an antechamber to hell, that weasel Valido would sell his soul to guarantee a book that brought him more prestige, more money, were I the devil and I would accept such a proposal, Valido is a good servant of the occult powers, a hellish weasel, no, this smell isn't normal, I feel a chill down my back, it could be a draft caused by the movement of the door, or just another incomprehensible thing, this place has bad vibrations, ah, Helena, if you were here and I told you this, you'd laugh at me, I'm so silly, yes, I've lost my outer conscience, now who will teach me to tell right from wrong?, it certainly won't be Valido, I look around and place my umbrella in a very dirty stand, the house is full of dust, it makes my nose itch, none of this is improving my poor health, my throat and lungs are affected, my body a battlefield, *kartofler*, by Zeus, this keeps coming up, there's something nasty here, I didn't like the way the old woman with the wart was looking at me on the streetcar and, now that I think of it, the woman looked like a witch, it's grotesque, a man gets himself entangled in obscure situations just by using these means of public transportation, I'll start taking more walks, it's good exercise, it helps air out all the grease from Mrs. Lucrécia's meals . . . now there's a good match for Valido, Mrs. Lucrécia, they're two misers of the highest class, one day I should introduce them, and here comes the secretary, she's fixing her hair, her bangs seem to disturb her, they irritate the soft skin on her forehead: it can happen, I've heard of such cases.

"Dr. Valido can see you now. Please follow me."

I follow her . . . Dr. Valido!, for Heaven's sake, the man is so entitled as to be referred to as Doctor like the student living in the room next to mine, and the audacity of announcing he can see me, as if he had his day occupied with hearings, the great King Solomon himself, in this city one can do nothing without previously consulting Dr. Valido, the genius, this man hasn't installed electricity in his office because he himself is working on a revolutionary electric system of his own creation, his feats are known overseas, oh no, in this country people are not valued, these mental skills aren't supported, the secretary moves away and closes the door behind me, I'm left before this contemporary Prometheus, at least so I assume, because I can't see him, the room is almost entirely pitch black, books pile up in columns taller than a man, at the end of the room I discern a desk.

"Mr. Valido?"

"Yes, yes, come closer."

Weary, I take a few steps forward, assuming he is sitting at his desk, I feel terribly startled when he appears from behind a column of books, bloody hell, the man is surely a servant of diabolic entities, the smell of sulfur intensifies.

"Jesus! I didn't see you in all this darkness."

The weasel smiles; at least I think it's a smile, a sneer that makes his face contract. His glasses have slipped to the tip of his nose, they're clearly too loose, he must have bought them at the street market, I bet he doesn't know if the lenses are the right prescription, he's holding a miniscule candle.

"Ah yes, light is bad for my eyesight, I'm a very fragile person." Yes, it might do some damage to your wallet too. "But please, do sit down."

He walks to the desk and sits on a chair, I can see only his head, I try to find a chair though I see only piles of books and papers, the candle burns on the desk, he looks at me in silence, waiting for me to take a seat, I don't see a single chair, therefore I sit on a huge heap of rather hefty looking books, he looks pleased.

"I'm delighted that you've accepted my request."

"You're welcome, Mr. Valido. It's a pleasure."

"I shall cut to the chase, I don't want to waste your time."

It crosses my mind to recline on the chair, my back hurts, I deter myself just in time when I remember I'm sitting on books, what's this under my legs, good gracious, the book covers are ghastly, they say Valido forces his daughter to design them together with the typographer, the miser can't afford anything better, he probably has a great deal of expenses with his offspring, he's a man who expects to profit from his investments, these are the individuals who make the world progress, their efforts are often praised, who am I to criticize them, I'll just sit here, I'm a mere translator in the dark, in any case you can't see the grease spots on my tie, the badger proceeds, he's sparing with words, one does not easily lose certain economic habits.

"It came to my knowledge that you've translated a book for Dr. Szarowsky's publishing house; am I right?"

"Yes, indeed, I've translated a book from the *Battle* series. The first volume."

"Yes, that's exactly the one I mean. Well, I've been told that the translation has been on hold for approximately two years, so I've contacted the author, who informed me that Dr. Szarowsky hasn't fulfilled his part of the contract, thus losing all rights related to the work in question. Therefore, I've acquired the rights to that internationally acclaimed and magnificent series."

"My congratulations on such an expeditious endeavor, Mr. Valido."

The weasel attempts a smile, another disgusting sneer, his face contorts in wrinkles, he looks like a dry fig. I hate the book, in fact, I loathe all the books in the series, art also goes through strange trends, wears its ostrich feather hats, wigs, face powder, none of which will go down in history, the book is teeming with banalities and disgraceful situations, it does nothing to enrich literature, but a man has to earn a living.

"You'll ask yourself, my friend, why I'm telling you all this. It's very simple: I've been told you've completed that translation, and since I intend to release the series in the very near future, I would like to acquire it. With this purpose in mind, I've talked with Dr. Szarowsky, who has agreed on my proposal."

"Yes, but . . ." this chit-chat annoys me terribly, I want to get up and set things in motion, just look at this filthy scum, I'd love to topple all these heaps of paper, turn over the desk, I close my fists, he opens his mouth.

"Yes?"

"Mr. Szarowsky's publishing house hasn't paid me what it owes me in over two years."

The weasel reclines on his creaking chair. The candle flame flickers.

"My, what an inconvenience. I have already paid Dr. Szarowsky and he told me everything was in order!"

"Yes, but I can assure you that it's not."

"I assume you can speak with Dr. Szarowsky directly."

"Yes, I will have to. And I would also like to give you a copy of the translation, since Mr. Szarowsky takes too many liberties with other people's work, as if he knew the original language, he of all people, who decides to publish books without reading them, not taking the trouble of even glancing at them. You wouldn't believe it if I told you that he wanted me to erase all references to snow, because no such phenomenon occurs in our own climate, perhaps he wanted me to use rain instead . . ."

"I appreciate it immensely, but the work is already being prepared for printing at the typographer's."

There's absolute silence. The weasel looks like a dry fig, and an excessively shriveled one too, the dry fig everybody disregards until it's the only one left on the table. A sheer aberration.

"Anything else?" I ask.

"Yes, yes, certainly. I would like you to translate the subsequent tomes. I'd like to discuss prices—according to what I've been told, your prices are quite reasonable (the dry fig smiles with pleasure)— and deadlines. I want to make sure I give you a more extended deadline than the one you had for the first translation. We could talk soon, very soon . . . perhaps tomorrow, same time?"

"Yes, of course."

The candle is almost out, I think of Szarowsky, that presumptuous fellow, a disgusting deadbeat, he robbed me of hours of life and didn't pay, if he had paid me I might now be on a ship, who knows, paying after such a long time is like not paying at all, ah, there's no justice in this country, the dry fig clears his throat, I understand there's nothing else left to say, I get up and reach out my hand.

"Mr. Valido, I'll see you tomorrow. It was a pleasure."

"The pleasure was all mine."

I shake his slimy hand, it's dry and wet at the same time, a mummified reptile's hand, he exerts no strength whatsoever, his fingers are like goo, limp, I've always had a bad impression about people who don't shake hands properly, they're disloyal, they hide their strength, they're niggardly, sluggish, impotent, perverts, their natural habitat is the sulfurous ether from the swamps, there's that smell of sulfur again, this is too much for an honest man to handle, it's indeed an antechamber of hell, I want to wipe my hand on my trousers, on paper, anything, I try to control myself, wait until I leave this den, the weasel wants to go back to his lair, I open the door, the candle flame flickers, I nod one last time in his direction, he answers in the same fashion, I close the door, walk past the secretary, who is sitting, she's still fixing her bangs, madam, don't wear that hairdo, it doesn't suit everybody, I tell her good afternoon, take my umbrella, she stands up from the chair, but I'm quicker and get out before she reaches me.

Oh, the fresh air, the muddy street, I reach into my pocket to get a cigarette, however, I only have matches, my keys and an orange, forgot to buy tobacco, I prefer the puddles of water outside to the mold inside the den, I feel a shiver going down my back again, must check out what's wrong, it's either my lungs or something nasty, I need some advice from Helena, I wonder what she might be doing now, is she reading in her cabin, looking at the sea over the bulwark, what might she be doing?, I have to go to Szarowsky's office to demand my money, it will help in buying the house, I can pay the first installment, then I'll be able to send her a letter explaining everything, I might even ring her, if she can receive phone calls, if they have a phone there, snow can knock down the lines, it's a hard life, I head toward another den of ignominy.

V

I wander about the city, I know the address by heart given the numerous times I've been there to demand my money, haven't been there in months, I'd lost hope of being paid, everything's an utter disgrace in this country, there's no civility, neither honesty nor respect, nothing indeed, everything's rotten, I'm walking along the long cobblestoned street, there are fruit stalls on both sides, all I see are apples, pears, and oranges, such a dull sight, an unbelievable monotony, not even these stands bring a dash of color to this dismal land, I arrive at the building where a nice bronze plaque reads "Dr. Szarowsky, Lawyer."

I lift my umbrella and ring the bell with its tip, I wait a moment, the door is opened by a young secretary, that pig-headed Szarowsky uses his facilities simultaneously for his work as a lawyer and as a publisher, nevertheless he still hasn't managed to pay what he owes me, the disgraceful parasite, it's not as if he doesn't have enough to eat, I have to live off Mrs. Lucrécia's peas while he travels all around the world, knows all the spas, all the cities and ruins, eats like a king, smokes imported cigars, I have to work by candlelight, while he only pretends to work in an office fully lit by electric light, he's loaded with money, this building looks like one of those fine hotels, a real luxury, the secretary shows me in.

"Wait a moment, please. I'll check if Dr. Szarowsky can see you now."

It seems they all have very busy schedules, I don't understand how it is that I never get to see anyone when I call on them, I must have flawless aim as far as timing is concerned, it might be a sign of witchcraft, spells, charms, I smell a curious odor again, it's not sulfur, the demon working here is of a different ilk altogether, it's in fact the smell of burning, this looks like too big a coincidence, one hides in sulfurous darkness, the other flaunts himself under a scorching light, it smells of burning corpses, souls broiling in the underworld, maybe in Tartar, or in Hades, the souls roam around oblivious, devoid of memory, that would explain a lot, no wonder Szarowsky forgot about his debts, Szarowsky, poor man, he works in Hades, I put the umbrella in the stand, it's still dry, in all this light the bloody deadbeat might look askance at my tie and I'm not even wearing a hat, what would you say if you saw me now, Helena, you left only a few hours ago and I'm already in this woeful state, I've probably caught a serious disease, the secretary returns, I fix my tie.

"Dr. Szarowsky will see you now. Please follow me."

All the rooms are lit, there are no scattered books here, everything looks sophisticated, I enter the illustrious editor's office and the secretary, who has some resemblance to a hen, leaves, I have no idea why, but she reminds me of a gallinaceous bird, maybe it's her dewlap, Szarowsky stands up prissily, the man's incapable of bending over, has had a stick glued to his spine since he was a small lad, there's no other reasonable explanation, he greets me with clear signs of fastidiousness, his eyes stare forever at my tie, one of the corners of his mouth twitches, he's upset, but that's only to be expected, here I am, disturbing him in his particular Hades, presenting myself with a soiled tie, there's an intense smell of burning in this room, I wonder if someone scorched bread recently, Szarowsky fixes his blond hair, he thinks he's irresistible, a god of beauty, this man is preposterous.

"Please, take a seat, my dear friend. So, what brings you here?"

The base imbecile asks what brings me here, as if there weren't more than enough reasons to visit him every day until he dies, disgraceful parasite, thief, he steals work and life from people and still comes across as an important member of the literati, a big shot, is surrounded by toadies who think he's extremely careful with the visual quality of the books he publishes, content doesn't matter, it never did, in fact, oh, I'm such an ass, I never knew which way the wind was blowing, or maybe I did, but I didn't want to follow it, all my life fighting against the current, nonetheless, they were the ones who have triumphed, I'm the amateur, these stupid dandies gather at parties, stuff their mouths with *hors d'oeuvres* as if they hadn't eaten in ages, miserable scoundrels, the public applauds, they couldn't care less if the publisher is in debt with the translator, the typographer, the cleaning lady, it's none of their business, pigs triumph.

"I've just met Mr. Valido, the publisher. He told me he has acquired the *Battle* series and purchased my translation from you. I don't object to that at all, however, as you will certainly understand, I still haven't received a centavo for my work. Mr. Valido is apparently convinced that everything is in order, according to what you have told him, when, in fact, I wasn't informed by you of this development, I was kept in the dark . . ."

While I speak, Szarowsky shifts his weight in the chair, he looks restless, though he maintains an upright posture at all times, he's a very prim man, he's holding a cigar but hasn't offered me one, there's a glass of wine on the desk though I'm not even allowed to drink a glass of water, another miser!, he gets to be very well paid, but is a real skinflint, the fool thought he'd get rich by publishing half a dozen books, it's a well-known fact, he has said in several conversations that he would make a fortune in this business, what an utter dimwit, the only solution would be an unerring shot to the head, so many war casualties and these lowlife beings were left here to pester the world, presumptuous idiot, he's a lawyer, therefore he knows justice doesn't work, I tried suing him for the debt and in the end he laughed . . . in my face!, we lose money in legal procedures and that's it, the judge is ill, the president is overthrown, the swindlers laugh . . . pure banter . . . in this country we're still living in the Stone Age, he drags himself to the edge of the chair and interrupts me.

"My dear friend, you are absolutely right, it has been an unforgivable oversight on my part. I've been swamped with work, my secretary was sick, my dear mother-in-law has passed away, oh well, I went through a series of misfortunes that ended up affecting my job. But don't you worry," he opens the desk drawer, "for we shall sort this out immediately. How much do I owe you?"

I open my mouth to speak, he lifts his hand and proceeds:

"I have a note with the amount here somewhere, I'll search for it right now . . . Yes, here it is, I knew I had it close by. I'm going to write you a check and the whole affair will be over in the most extraordinary fashion."

The imbecile signs the check and hands it to me over the desk, it might bounce, the banks are already closed but I shall cash it tomorrow morning, just look at this, he even managed to steal a couple of centavos from me, nonetheless I won't be bothered with this any longer, the mere sight of his face nauseates me, there's a smell of burning here, it's satanic, I notice that Szarowsky is not his last name, in fact, he has three more family names after that, the slow-wit uses this one to sound fancier, what a snob, the other names are ordinary, one has to be very presumptuous to do something like that, the pig-headed deadbeat is a true product of our society, ah, how he rejoices in wallowing in the mud. I refuse to thank him, he's the one who should beg on his knees for my forgiveness and pay interest.

"Right," I put the folded check in my breast pocket, protected by the coat. "Well, it's been a pleasure. I won't take up any more of your time."

I get up, the lawyer stands as if he had a plumb line secured to his neck, still holding his cigar.

"I hope you'll hold no grudges! You must understand things have not gone as expected, I tried to reconcile this passion with advocacy, and it wasn't easy. However, we've tried to do something new, to reinvent the present literary canon . . . an important task, in fact, as significant as determining the biblical canon."

Reinvent the canon, the literary canon! And he talks about the significance of the biblical canon! My God, if I'd have been carrying a weapon, I'd have ruined my life!

"You do understand this situation, don't you? You deal with so many professionals in this business, you are aware of how we've made a clear difference. Anyway, we will continue following that path, our mission isn't over yet. And I'll tell you what: I'm going to recommend you to other potential clients and let you know should I need your services in the future for matters related to my law practice," he brings the cigar to his mouth; he never lit it. "Yes, we're trying to reinvent the canon!"

That hideous fair head . . . and the cigar in his mouth is the pinnacle of horror, terror lives a golden age within these premises, I have entered the realm of the great beast from hell, there's a smell of burning, I only want the money so that I can buy a new house, new curtains, a bit of paint for the frames, perhaps do some restoration work on the inside, what am I doing in front of this repulsive creature, this is too much for an honest man, I feel a pain in my chest, I miss her, melancholy invades me, he looks at me with his swine-like eyes.

"Mr. Szarowsky . . ."

"Yes?"

"*Kartofler, kartofler, kartofler.*"

It looks like Szarowsky received an electric shock, maybe some sort of interference from the electric light so elegantly displayed in the room, it resembles a palace, he's the Sun King, he sucks on his cigar wide-eyed, he doesn't know what to say, so there, now you too will have something rattling in your head, now try sleeping as you wonder what this might mean, reinvent your sweet canon as many times as it pleases you, yes, laugh a little bit, and look, here we have a pile of paper, how about I give it a tumble?, the sheets of paper all scattered on the floor . . . there it goes . . . a slight touch was enough, the sheets of paper spread over the floorboards, Dr. Szarowsky's lacking sense of order is to blame for this mess, he stares at the pieces of paper with amazed eyes, I turn my back on him and open the door and then close it immediately, I never look back and move forward with large steps to the stand, grab my umbrella, the secretary who looks like a hen starts getting up, I tell her not to bother, look for my hat, but then I remember I no longer have one; when I open the front door, Szarowsky simultaneously opens his office door and shows his golden head, which shines under the light coming from the numerous chandeliers.

"What did you say? *Klitofer?*"

His repugnant monkey head trapped between the door and the frame, now that would make an excellent spectacle.

"*Kartofler*, Mr. Szarowsky. It requires a certain refinement to pronounce it."

I close the door, the office disappears like magic, the smell of burning is now but a memory, I enjoy the fresh air, he must still be confused, I don't restrain my smile, the street welcomes me again with its puddles, it's too late to go to the bank, I can't just knock at the door of the yellow house to talk to the owner, it's probably an old woman, she won't open the door for me in this light and I wouldn't be able to take a proper look at the property anyway, nonetheless it's too early for dinner, so I decide to stop at the café.

VI

Evening is falling down upon me, the afternoon quickly faded out, it ran away from the rain, which in fact never arrived despite its promises, I take my dear umbrella for a stroll, it's a useful object whenever I need help crossing muddy streets, ringing doorbells, or presenting myself as neat, a providential item now that I've lost my hat, the soiled tie is a true blemish on my attire, it was exposed to ridicule in the intensely lit Szarowsky's office, that gigantic swine, he can keep his *kartofler* in his head, let it resound within his dim skull, at long last I have a check well hidden in my breast pocket, anyway, tomorrow I'll look for my hat in the streetcar company's lost and found office, I'll go to the central station, doubt I'll find it there, the garlic woman left it on the seat just to be snatched or squeezed under a monstrous bottom, the toothless kid took it so he can use it in his perverted childish games, everything's possible, I'll investigate this business thoroughly, want to know its whereabouts, this check isn't enough to suddenly make me feel like a wealthy man who can scatter hats around downtown, dusk brings a growing cold with it, a chilly wind's blowing, I shiver under my coat, which is still a bit wet, I'm going to get sick, but it'll all be worth it if I manage to buy that house, she will return, this miserable life spent in rented rooms will end, as well as the smell of stews and roasts in other people's homes, the ever-occupied toilet will be a thing of the past, what a nuisance to cross our backyard in the rain to find the privy door closed and the student sleeping inside, how absurd, we live in a medieval country, there's no hygiene, I wander through the streets and see nothing but excrement and litter on the ground, I almost slip on an apple peel, it occurs to me to rummage in my pocket, the orange is still where I've put it, I've nearly reached the café, only a few yards left to get there, the café is well lit, it's quite dark outside, soon the streetlamps will be turned on, it smells of tar, this city is infested with hellish odors, it needs to be fumigated, disinfected, it harbors too many rats, I see some people sitting at the tables, I go in, leave my umbrella in the stand, look around, get used to the faint light from the wall lamps, one hand is waving in the air, someone calls me, yes, one man with a woman by his side, I can't escape any-more, Teodorico and Hermengarda have already seen me, they're expecting me to join them at their table, I get closer, greet them, I pull out a chair, sit down and touch my shirt, the check is still here, the waiter asks me what I'd like to order, I order a tea, there's a big beer tankard in front of Teodorico, Hermengarda is herself facing a dessert plate with an unknown cake on it, two large slices, dough spitting out cream, it's repulsive, I turn my face, Teodorico starts talking while smoking, he exhales smoke and words, it's obvious he feels no shame for his bad breath, I notice he doesn't take proper care of his oral hygiene, his teeth are sinister, probably spends all his spare time combing and fixing his forelock and the scarf he wears around the neck, I think he even ties it with several knots before he lies down to sleep, I have to strain to hear him.

"We were just talking about you. What a joyful coincidence!"

"You know what they say: speaking of the devil . . ."

"Yes, yes! That's funny," Hermengarda has the awful habit of talking in every circumstance, even when she has nothing to say, she suffers from a serious disease, she's a show-off and therefore feels the need to apply an exuberance of make-up on her small round face, she pretends to be prettier than she is but she doesn't fool me, oh no, she's friends with everyone, smiles and talks and is fond of them all, loves one fellow and at the same time loves his foe, how I despise neutrality, only countries should be neutral since they're abstract entities, people cannot be neutral, a friend of mine cannot caress my hand and kiss my enemy, laugh when they mock me, this is my true belief, maybe I'm wrong, neutral people are the most dangerous, they sell themselves to the highest bidder, betray us for a plate of lentils, I advocate for oranges and their cultivation, want to spread orangeries throughout the country, but a good-for-nothing idiot thinks they should be eradicated, so, faced with two different perspectives, these neutral people consider both points of view valid without commit-ting themselves to either, Hermengarda would laugh and support the cultivation of oranges and simultaneously their extinction, when asked for her opinion she closes her mouth tight, she can't man-age to be honest, will never say she hates something, maybe she's not even honest to herself, perhaps I'm too bold, but these fellows are disgusting, rats from the sewers, they take advantage of every chance to climb up, she can smell opportunity from far away, she hangs out with everyone, ugly and handsome alike, tall and short, good and bad, she has no values, anything suits her as long as she can gain something from it, she repels all her suitors for fear of losing her charm and radiance after she's engaged, men try to conquer her, they share the hope of taking her, they're abject, they behave like youngsters and can't understand they'll never get their wishes, there are no limits for these men, they're immoral perverts, base, our sweet Hermengarda isn't stupid at all, she knows which way the wind blows, she's quite different from me in that matter, puts her social skills to use, she wants to be a writer, God!, one more poet, in this country everyone is a poet, I shouldn't have come to the café, for now I notice a little notebook in front of Teodorico, he's a poet too, I sense I will endure some pain.

"And did you speak highly or ill of me?"

"Highly, my dear friend, as always! We were talking about your translation, the one to be published this month . . . Valido didn't lose any time, indeed. And they say the series' second volume will be released in two months' time. Isn't that so?"

"In two months! Impossible!" Such a thick book as that!, I haven't yet begun to translate it, there's something foul in this, I smell the sulfurous odor again. "Might it be true . . . ? Where did you hear such a thing?"

Teodorico strokes his beard and exhales more tobacco smoke, I can't see his face for some seconds, I cough and can't breathe, Hermengarda smiles stupidly at my side.

"I cannot recall with certainty who first told me, but people are saying it all around. In bookstores, cafés . . ."

"So, the second volume is due to be released in two months, is that it?"

"Yes, exactly, even booksellers are confirming the release date, this book is dreadfully expected, you see. I guess it was Valido himself who spread the rumors to ease the readers' anxiety. He's a true master of publishing, knows what he's doing."

Indeed he knows . . . masters and commanders, in this den they all are masters and commanders, no doubt a result of living in such a mountainous and sea-beaten country, from the rocky peaks one can, with no effort, contemplate miles and miles of land, thousands of trees, millions of people, libraries and rooms full of books, truth be told, there's no other occupation for a noble spirit than that of being a master or a commander of publishing and similar arts, and they do it with the utmost delicacy . . . from the mountain tops . . . in a refreshing fashion, I can even feel the wind tickling me.

"Nice to know it, thank you for the news."

"Ah, you're playing humble! You know all this better than me. Perhaps you intended to keep it a secret for some more time, huh?"

"Yes, perhaps, but I'm only a translator, I know nothing, as always! Nothing, I tell you!"

"If you write a book one day, I'll be the first to buy it. You're so witty," says the young woman.

"Yes, I'm wittiness personified, so much so that sometimes I present my very own one-man show, a prodigious spectacle, a man inside a tent, but there's no tent, only a man, and people enjoy it nevertheless, a few get in fact the bizarre notion of throwing me coins, bank notes . . . think about it, they want to pay me."

Hermengarda laughs like a school girl, she squeezes my arm, with the other hand she touches Teodorico, she's shameless, if we were alone and I a publisher or a writer, she would be sitting on my lap by now, what a smart little seducer, no, she won't pull it off with me, my Helena left on a ship, what do I want these women for, they're not worth a single hair of hers, at any rate, for what purpose would she want to seduce me, I'm a wretched man, I'm wearing a greasy tie and, in the name of Zeus, I'm a tramp, I lack the necessary sophistication to rub elbows with these individuals, I present myself in disarray, dirty, hatless! However, that will change, I'll buy my own house, stop eating peas and mushy rice, no one deserves the life I've been living, I will get rid of all the idiots, Szarowsky has already disappeared from my sight, the big presumptuous fool took a surname from a grandmother, some poor maid, he was certainly conceived on a hay bale, in the stables, the horses neighed during the few minutes of feverish passion, I will get another hat, rest assured, Teodorico stares at Hermengarda, he tries to stifle his laughter to prove he didn't find my remarks funny at all, this bum is a boot-licker, a sellout, he too would like to share intimate moments with this adventurer by my side . . . intimate moments and opinions on literature . . . on art . . . however, they can barely read, at the most they've read some excerpts from the Bible and now they see them-selves as poets, God, I'm surrounded by animals, they bray and caw, it's a true farmhouse, she proceeds:

"You're a blasphemous man, but I don't care. To be honest, I'm quite liberal on religious issues and I've an interest in almost every-thing, my curiosity knows no bounds and I'd love to travel, study, and read ceaselessly . . . if only I could live with no food! But, as I cannot, I try to learn as much as possible . . . with neither prejudice nor constraints. You see, I even tried to take our dear Teodorico to a fortune teller. He was afraid and refused to go in."

"I beg your pardon: it wasn't a fortune teller, but a witch."

"Right, Teodorico—fortune teller, witch, whatever you wish. I thought it's all the same to you, atheists," says Hermengarda. Teodorico often hides himself behind a thick smoke curtain. "Isn't it all a ludicrous trick played by charlatans?"

"Indeed, it is, but . . . I don't want to waste my precious time with shenanigans. Bah!"

"Maybe you want to pay her a visit," Hermengarda addresses me, Teodorico vanishes behind smoke, "she's got a practice nearby, she lives and works in an apartment over the hardware store, you know, the lame hardwareman whose store has a derelict sign plate passersby bump their head against, the one on the square."

"Yes, I see, I know the place you're talking about," I interrupt her little speech, her voice gets on my nerves, I decide to ask Teodorico for a cigarette, I gesture to him, bring an open hand to my mouth, he understands, nods, offers me a cigarette, I light it.

"Her name is Madame Rasmussen. But perhaps you don't want to go and, just like Teodorico, you're an atheist who's afraid of witches."

Teodorico is clearly annoyed with the conversation, maybe he fears the witch will punish him, or else he's only embarrassed, no one knows what he's thinking, it's impossible to tell, when one opens a man's head one cannot see but fluids and substances of dubious consistency, it would be wonderful if one could extract thoughts, it would make life easier, at least for the ones who opened heads, not so much for those who got opened, nonetheless it would be a glorious show, a lovely display . . . all the trepanations . . . *en masse* . . . performed outdoors . . . true public ceremonies, and in the end we would breathe easier, the world would be a more pleasant place.

"Certainly, I will stop by her office. Besides a certain anthropological interest in her line of work, I could use Madame Rasmussen's help, something that would do much to please me. I've been sensing curious smells, harmful sulfurous odors, it seems to me there's always something burning everywhere I go, yes, maybe that Madame of yours can tell me where those acidic, stinky fragrances come from."

"You're so witty!"

The young seducer laughs again, from her point of view everything's extremely funny, she disrespects others' problems, their personal dramas!, I'm surrounded by self-seekers and incompetents, only now does the waiter bring me my tea, they must have picked fresh tea leaves in Ceylon, a true classy service, the waiter puts the cup and the teapot on the table and turns his back to us, there's a moment of silence, Teodorico mulls over his shameful behavior, such a grown-up man afraid of visiting a fortune teller, it's a scandal, he's finished, he can throw his artistic aspirations into the ocean, Hermengarda rolls her eyes, she's probably pondering our conversation, she doesn't know if I was mocking her by saying I would call on Madame Rasmussen or not, I'm a serious man, I do not soil my mouth with frivolities, in this country only serious people triumph, all humor is cut off, stupid people can't deal with humor, they have some difficulty understanding irony, it's too subtle for their taste and, speaking about triumph and taste, Teodorico opens his small notebook, I foresee the worst-case scenario, this amazing poet will show me one more of his poems, the slice of cake is still on Hermengarda's plate, it seems she can't make up her mind about eating it, maybe her little hat is crushing her head, my tea is too hot, though at the moment that's advantageous for me, need assistance fighting the heartburn I'll be afflicted with after I read his poem, he makes himself ready, wets his lips, there's no escape for me.

"Let's forget all that story about witches, that's irrelevant. On the other hand, I've got a few poems of mine here and I'd like to know what you think of them," says Teodorico, and he pushes his open notebook over the table, it crosses the tabletop and almost topples the pot, Hermengarda grabs the little plate and finally makes up her mind about eating the slice of cake. "Perhaps I have some other better poems. But can you please read them?"

"Yes, of course."

I drink a sip of tea, it's still too hot, it burns my tongue, I look down at the open notebook, I immediately smell mud mixed with garbage and urine, don't know what's happening, I must inquire about this phenomenon, Madame Rasmussen might give me some satisfactory answers, doctors probably wouldn't know how to treat me, maybe she can also check if I suffer from a lung malady, I need to save money so I can buy that house, where is Helena now?, I stare at the piece of paper but can't read the words, I think about her, she's on the ship, what time is it in that exact location?, she can't have moved much forward, the ship is slow, extraordinarily slow, it will take a long time before I get a letter from her, it's excruciating, I try to focus on what is written in front of me, trite images of love, boring wordplays, dear Heavens, I'm not a specialist on poetry, but this is too much for a single man, I've not sinned against humanity, he loves profoundly a certain lady, once again something about love, now a strong wind, ceiling lamps swinging, a shot to the chest, straight through the heart, wound me and leave me to die, hit me in the flank, why not in the crotch?

"Say again?" asks Teodorico.

"Say again what?"

"You said something about a crotch, as I understood."

"Oh, nothing relevant, I was reading and began to think aloud. I'm going to resume reading, if you don't mind."

Hadn't noticed I was talking out loud, I sip some more tea, get back to the poem, try to focus, however, out of the corner of my eye, I see Hermengarda finishing her cake, she doesn't exactly eat it with finesse, Helena, you're much more delicate, one can't see you chewing, you don't drop crumbs, this woman is filthy, she chews the cud like a cow, her tongue sticking out, pigs are cleaner than her, why do they force pigs to live in their own filth?, they're unsoiled, humans are the worst creatures on earth's surface, damn hairless monkeys, disgusting, Teodorico stares absentmindedly at the ceiling, he pretends he's not interested in what's happening at the table though he's wringing his hands, it's pathetic, I continue to read, the torment is endless, I read and instantly forget what I read, these second-rate poets play with words but say nothing, nothing!, a token of pure spiritual misery, they scribble shamelessly and consider themselves poets, Hermengarda is even a worse writer than him, some perverted old men tell her she writes divinely, she's a natural-born poet, gifted, just try to get yourself engaged to someone and you'll see how much they care about your poetry, we live in a gross world, wallow in the mud, there are no friends, only self-seekers, they suck us dry, break our bones and gulp down the marrow, it's a delicacy, if your job is as so and so they remember you, if you stop working as so and so, they never acknowledge you, they're true thugs, if one travels abroad they're flattering, want to know where one's been traveling to, if one travels a few miles they're not in the least interested, they want to know nothing, even if one's seen a dragon spitting fire over a stunning landscape, these people cherish mere shells, the pretend-to-be illusions of their peers, they live with inner traumas never dealt with, I'm no different, I'm part of this cursed species, I was born a man, cannot stop being who I am, maybe I can, at the most, be less a man and a bit more a person, oh, the love Teodorico feels once again, lamps blown by the wind, swinging to and fro, it's despicable, let the lamps alone, the light, the stars, now he sews stars to the sky's black cloth, metaphors that nearly bring tears to my eyes, what smell is this I'm sensing?, where does it come from, it's sulfur, there's something diabolic in these poems, perhaps they're merely bad, I don't know, many affirm they're good, am I the only normal person in this country or am I mistaken?, why was I born here, dear God, why did you have to punish me this way?, is it the original sin to blame?, Hell!, we're still paying for that little mistake, for my part I had nothing to do with it, I'm not guilty, I drink some more tea and leaf through the notebook, poems on insects, grasshoppers, and moths hovering above his beloved's hair, which opens itself like butterfly wings, now this is way too much, it's crossed the line, it bores me to sleep, they all are so intellectual, their grandparents certainly don't understand a single word of what they say, in this country there are two kinds of people, the overly intellectualized and the illiterate, there's no middle ground, I suffocate here, I wonder if I should buy that house or go away instead, it's too tiring, repulsive, don't want to hang out with these fellows, I'd rather talk to the walls, why must we work for a living?, I gulp down a mouthful of tea, I page back and forth through the notebook, I assemble some courage, wish to be honest.

"Well, these poems are . . ."

Teodorico leans forward over the table, he's anxious, I start to speak but then someone enters the café, they get distracted, it's the literary critic who writes for the newspapers, Hermengarda's eyes shine, one of her admirers has arrived, he's an old lady-killer, he hides his impotence under a fake gleefulness, his mature age weighs heavily on him, he's degrading himself, reached the basest level of existence, Hermengarda begins to stand, she doesn't do it though, must wait so he can sit down, Teodorico stares at him, follows his movements, he's now forgotten how he wanted to hear my opinions on his poetry, who am I to talk about literature, the critic is among us, he comments on books based on their author and not the content itself, some say he doesn't even read them, only a few pages, this way he can pretend, despite it being his sole occupation in life, he can't possibly read all those books, since he spends his days drooling over young women, a most grotesque situation, mankind's vilest scum, while they stare at him I manage to finish drinking my tea, the critic has taken a seat near the window, I say goodbye and get up, they answer me without moving a muscle, they grunt, it's as if I'm not here anymore, I give the waiter a coin, pay for my tea, leave the notebook full of poems on the table, what a relief, the burning sulfurous smell appears to be vanishing, I walk toward the front door, Teodorico and Hermengarda exchange a look, they've made their silent decision, they'll sit by the critic, they take care of their literary careers without writing, that's how the wind blows around here, in this country there are different natural laws, weird phenomena, how peculiar, we're primitive but there's no problem, they say our food is excellent, I know nothing about such a topic, I eat only peas floating on fat, food is crucial, it nourishes a person's soul, with good food one can bear everything, culture and education are secondary, we all want the same, I want to have a house, want Helena, I have neither, I grab my umbrella and leave, when walking in front of the big window I see the three of them sitting together, Hermengarda laughs joyfully, I turn around, shrug, still need to walk all the way home, it's dark outside, the streetlamps are lit, my stomach roars, the tea I drank didn't satiate my hunger, the dinner prepared by Mrs. Lucrécia awaits me in our grim dwelling.

VII

It starts raining when I'm almost home, in fact it's merely drizzling, nonetheless it's quite annoying, once more the drops fall like pins on my eyes, the past would repeat itself if I didn't have my umbrella, tomorrow I shall look for the lost hat before meeting the revolting Valido, so the miser intends to have the translation published in two months, I must get to the bottom of this matter as soon as possible, I wonder what his intentions are, either he wants me to work without sleeping or I'm not going to translate the book, oh, that beguiler, weasel, he loves to worm information out of people, why would he call me to his office if he didn't want to hire me?, one never knows what's on these idiots' minds, there's no logic with them, *kartofler*, they are parasites, what does a parasite think about?, they latch onto their hosts and suck, truth be told, they can't think much in those circumstances, Valido is a proglottid, yes, that's it, I won't mention Szarowsky, who doesn't even get to be an amoeba, what a disgrace, pure intellectual baseness, I walk the last few yards under an open umbrella, there's no light coming out from the windows, the crone probably lit only one wretched candle, they all are inside, I know it, it's almost dinner time, the scheduled hour of bliss, there's the smell of stew in the air, damn gravy, I have stomachaches in the night, dinner drops like a plum in my belly, in this house one eats only fat, it's a crying shame, I fold my umbrella, feel some rain drops on my neck while fumbling for the key, then open the door, I come into the gloomy entrance hall, can hear dishes rattling in the kitchen, Mrs. Lucrécia shouts at the maid, poor girl, she works in a kitchen partly inhabited by a hippo, I put my umbrella in the stand, I close the door, darkness deepens, only the light coming in from the skylight brightens the staircase, as usual I climb up two steps at a time, the corridor is dead silent, I see some light in the transom above Miss Sancha's door, she's waiting for the dinner call, from my neighbor's room comes neither sound nor visible signs of life, he might have gone out to study the bottom of some glasses, let him study, he too knows how the wind blows, only I didn't know it, so much intelligence and so little cunning, I'm an idiot, can't learn anything, why do I have convictions that lead me to failure?, I wish I could be social with everyone, be a neutral person, I'd be a hypocrite but I'd be in a better situation by now, not in a chilly dark room, eating Mrs. Lucrécia's stews, Helena would be at my side, she'd never love a man like all others, she's no ordinary woman, she's above all these petty things, nevertheless I'd have to be a man like the others to give her what she'd like to have, I'm facing a complex dilemma, or maybe my hungry mind sees it as complex, I step into my room, it's unpleasantly cold, the light from streetlamps comes diffusely in through my window, I take off my coat, hang it on a rack, open the drawer in which I hide Helena's scarf, breathe in its fragrance, finally an agreeable odor!, I forget the sulfur, the garbage, I'll ask Madame Rasmussen some advice on my olfactory problems, someone shall be wise enough to help me, I long to talk to the yellow house's owner, I assume it's a woman, yes, it must be an old widow, where are you now?, the high seas must be dreadful at night, one can't see a thing, perhaps only stars, this if the sky is not cloudy, I put the scarf back in, sit down at the desk, on which many sheets of paper are scattered, have to translate some business letters, there's still time, at the moment I'm not inclined to work, wouldn't focus on the job, there are too many ideas spinning in my head, I overthink, I fear I shall endure a restless night, tossing and turning in bed never falling asleep, I hear footsteps in the corridor, the staircase boards creak, Miss Sancha's probably going downstairs, to the dining room, hideous!, another day in my life ends and I'm still part of a stew, I'm a pea floating on gravy, when will I be swallowed?, I get up, don't light the candle, see myself in the mirror, I forgot to look for the meaning of *kartofler*, how is it possible to have forgotten such a disturbing issue?, it seems I can't manage to recall it, I'm sure it's some triviality, I'm senile!, and the screams . . . good Heavens, Mrs. Lucrécia will still look askance at me, she was surprised by such a scene, an affront to good old practices, my face near hers, doing so to a decent lady is an act of sheer terror, I fix my tie and hair, I'm well groomed, I hear my landlady tapping on the tureen with a spoon, dinner is served.

I leave the room, fumble my way down the pitch-black stairs, my eyes take a long time to adjust to different levels of shadows, I cough once, twice, disease is spreading throughout my whole body, I should eat a garlic clove to ward off the flu, it could actually be pneumonia, I'll end up in a sanatorium, I'll die in an anonymous bed, a sad end indeed, the living will still eat stews, write poetry, drive streetcars, if that's my destiny, it would be preferable to give up soon, I'd rather be torn up in pieces right now, ground by bombs and shrapnel and bullets and barbed wire, die instantly, like a man, instead of dying little by little, yielding, day after day, to death, we strive to be someone, to live, work, own a house, eat, be a writer, a translator, and for what purpose?, we all die sooner or later, the world doesn't stop spinning, we only postpone the inevitable, why are we compelled to fight for our survival?, if she was here with me it would be worth it, however, she's not, it's a calamity, I enter the dining room, it's lit by a triple candlestick, there are three of us at the table, the student didn't show up, Mrs. Lucrécia serves Miss Sancha, I cannot tell for sure what's the dish served as dinner, but it seems to consist of lentils and potatoes, I presume!, it's a strange gravy, the vapors again, do I smell burning?, one can hear pans and pots rattling in the kitchen, the maid is tidying and cleaning, she's not allowed to dine together with us.

"Good evening, my ladies."

"Good evening," they say in unison, almost as if rehearsed beforehand.

"Mrs. Lucrécia, you're still looking ethereal like a Valkyrie—and Miss Sancha fresh as a nymph, of course."

"Always so gallant! But please sit down, I'll serve you immediately."

Miss Sancha begins to talk about her day in the office, her boss ordered a new typewriter, as far as I understand it's a big event, she doesn't know how to use it, her boss is going to teach her, one of the other employees is pregnant, happy times, it seems, Mrs. Lucrécia rejoices at the news and shows herself interested while filling my plate with potatoes and the mysterious stew, then proffers me the plate, oh yes, I was not mistaken, it's lentil stew, too watery, I see, the lentils float on gravy and almost jump out of the plate, I struggle not to spill food on my tie, Mrs. Lucrécia helps herself to olive oil, she's still staring at Miss Sancha, maybe she's trying to avoid me, the bizarre scene on the stairs before lunch disturbed her, she might never recover from the shock, I'm obscene, Miss Sancha pushes food to and fro on her plate while speaking, has slender fingers, I take a drink of water, the dining room is cold, food has not yet warmed me, the potatoes are too soft, they've melted, Mrs. Lucrécia swallows everything, seeing her eating is a circus show, repulsive, she's a paragon of ludicrousness, she chews, and bits of potato run down her oiled chin, the candle flames quiver. I closely observe both women, don't listen to what they say, I think I can hear myself chewing, am I making too much noise?

"Forgive me if my chewing bothers you. Am I being too noisy, perhaps?"

They say nothing . . . I look down at my plate, chew, they resume their conversation, I feel as if I'm outside my body, I'm alive and don't know if I'm alive, don't know if I'm dreaming, if I exist, for a few moments that's how I feel, it happens sometimes, I require something outside of me to confirm my existence, then I get back to a normal state, in those occasions I don't know if I shall continue to move, talk, if I don't exist, why should I do it?, despite that I proceed down the same path just out of habit, otherwise there'd be time lapses, I miss her, my expectations of receiving a letter are high with anxiety, the post will take many days to arrive, an unbearable bestiality permeates our surroundings, these women talk and talk and do not perceive my anguish, I wonder if they can hear my jaw, its creaks and snaps, how is it possible to be so aloof, for my part I cannot pretend to know what they feel, we humans are always alone, intimacy can disturb me, I admit it, being too intimate with someone leads to an extreme shyness, one looks at and loves a certain body, nonetheless that body is outside oneself, it's painful to touch it, one's not ashamed of nudity, but of abandoning one's flesh, I could be dreaming, maybe I don't exist, touching is a meaningless and useless gesture, I live in fear, stuck between walls, I'm not chewing anymore, I take a long time doing it, forget to chew, lose myself in erratic thoughts, I know I'm once again chewing, swallowing, eating, yes, it's true, I hear nothing of what the women are saying, this light brings me to a state of utter despondency, the life-supporting high spirits present during daytime vanish, I'm upset, apathetic, my companions finish their meal, talk with each other, I want to yell, pierce the ceiling with my screams and shouts, however, I control myself, still!, I put down my knife and fork, my back hurts, I push my chair away from the table, want to sleep with her scarf at my side, I get up.

"My ladies, if you'll forgive me, I'm going upstairs."

"Already?" asks Mrs. Lucrécia. "So early?"

"Yes, I have a busy day tomorrow."

They bid me good night, I leave the dining room, climb the stairs, grab my room key, I need to wash myself, remove all the dirt, eliminate the dung smell ingrained in my pores, in my hair, and then I can lie down with your pure and sweet recollection as my companion.

VIII

I wake up, the scarf is at my side, I clutched it while sleeping, taking into account the faint light coming in, I conclude it's still early, I slept restlessly, tossed and turned in my bed, dreamlessly fell asleep just to daydream soon after, although most nightmares vanished from my memory, I do remember a moment in which I woke up sweating and kept myself in a torpor between consciousness and unconsciousness, Helena was aboard a sinking ship, the waters dragged her to a desolate, gray coastline, inhabited by seagulls and rocks, there were pebbles on the beach and she, barefoot, cut her toes, I arrived on the scene from inland, emerged from a hole, foes suddenly began to run out of the water, they were ordinary people, fellows I could find any day on a streetcar or in business offices, nevertheless, they ran with an angry look, they had swords in their hands, I was armed with a rifle onto whose muzzle I fixed a bayonet, then I started shooting, Helena disappeared from sight, I fired incessantly, my maimed and suffering enemies died and faded into thin air, they never reached me, I killed, cut them with the bayonet, shot, blood was spilled, I wanted to protect Helena but couldn't find her anymore, I did everything I could to save her, a pointless task, because she got tired of waiting for me, she didn't say it out loud but one could feel it, she simply ran away, and despite that I knew she was nowhere to be found, I proceeded to kill my enemies, I shot them in the head, chest, legs, I did it without moving an inch, rooted in the same spot, I fought every single one of them but did not move forward, didn't draw near Helena, it became clear that fighting for her was a lost cause, useless since she was not with me, nonetheless I persisted, no one helped me, I shot and shot until I finally woke up.

I raise myself on my elbow, the light is too faint to create a shadow of my profile on the wall over me, I don't know why I'm thinking about this sleepless dream, I've a sour taste in my mouth, tastes like iron, blood, a nasty hot liquid is burning my esophagus, the stew isn't sitting well, I put down the scarf, don't wish to soil it, these nightmares are awful, they disappear but leave behind an unstable, hidden feeling, I'd rather forget these dreams, exhaustion consumes me, I feel pain in my neck and am so sad as I lay down to sleep, I can't let melancholy weigh me down, I'll have a busy day, can't even waste time by eating breakfast and sharing kind words with my illustrious neighbors, I'll leave home as soon as I wash and get dressed, I don't need food, I'm self-sufficient, indestructible, those nightmares mean nothing to me, they're mere brain contractions, a loose and irrational imagination connecting memories and wishes, I've read about it in one of the magazines I've translated, these scientific theories are interesting but I won't exclude more traditional explanations, our ancient common knowledge, the darkest arts, will ask Madame Rasmussen her opinion on the matter, I intend to secure her wise assistance today, I will pay a visit to her premises, Hermengarda can wait to join me until the cows come home, I have neither patience nor time for her kind, I jump out of bed, face the coldness, put on some clean long johns, it would be nice to get back my hat, the streetcar central station is not far from the bank, I hastily get dressed, my clothes are so cold they seem wet, living in this house is quite disgusting, we have no heating, life's worse than in a cave, I wash my face, must break a thin layer of ice on the water, I comb in front of the mirror, must wear the same tie, the light coming in through the window is gradually getting brighter, I think it won't rain today, I put on my coat and confirm I still have the check in my shirt pocket, open the door and leave, walk lightly down the stairs, so Mrs. Lucrécia cannot hear me passing by, one can hear pans rattling in the kitchen, the maid's already working, from the student's room come strange sounds, groans of pain, the long hours of studying are no doubt harming his health, he strives too much, the door to my landlady's room creaks, I must hurry up, I avoid engaging in hollow conversation at so early an hour, fatuous flattery does not suit my current mood, I reach the entrance hall in safety, it's awfully dark here, I open the door with extreme care and am immediately struck by a draft, I get out onto the street and silently close the door behind me.

They're turning off the streetlamps, a small boy shouts trying to sell newspapers, I call him, give him a coin, take a look at the first page, distant wars, national political movements, another coup, workers beaten by the police, a banker ran away with his clients' money, a man enraged by jealousy stabbed his wife to death, the usual in this country, nothing about ships, I shall scrutinize this newspaper from its front to its last page, there's certainly no relevant tragedy to report, I dirty my hands with ink, I roll the newspaper and put it under my arm, it's a chilly morning, my vaporous breath hovers in the air, since I don't have a cigarette with which to occupy myself, I create these white steamy clouds, I walk to the streetcar stop, people run to and fro, the teamsters pull their mules forward, the automobile drivers honk their horns, they want passersby to move away as fast as possible, they're true savages, madmen, there's no respect or civility, this country is a pigsty, can't even be considered a sovereign state, it's a patchwork, a ragged cloth worn down by time, it still lives on illusions of a glorious past, a land inhabited by a people more willing to move than to change, that is how we live around here, I'm this race's offspring, I like this country but I don't like this country, I lose myself in fairy tales, demented thoughts, I try to change something that will never change, it's impossible, improvements clash directly with the nation's essence, Helena understood all this a long time ago, she knows it, should I buy that house?, yes, it's the only solution, we need to cling to something, keep hope alive, the little yellow house is a horse bit in my mouth, it holds my tongue tight and I allow it, for it's the only course of action I can follow, the streetcar halts, people gather in front of the doors, I board it with ease, intentionally keep myself at the back, when I pay for my ticket the vehicle is already full, there are no empty seats left, I stay by a door, the streetcar heads off in fits and starts, the city landscape passes by me though I don't actually pay attention to it.

Some passengers talk, others laugh, might it be that one of them is in possession of my hat?, I do not know, don't look up, don't have enough strength to do it, am too lazy, I prefer the whirling moments of ignorance before having an epiphany of the epiphany itself, the air coming in through the glassless windows freezes my face, I stick both hands in my coat pockets, the orange is still here, I had forgotten its existence and will eat it later, I'm not hungry, lost my appetite once she told me about her departure, I eat the bare minimum to stay alive, have no sense of taste, nor am I a glutton, the streetcar stops but no one gets out, all the passengers are traveling toward downtown, people waiting on the sidewalk shout and try to come in, however, the driver doesn't let them in, he drives at full speed, the rails groan and cry for help, this monstrous mutt is killing us with its weight, they say, please save us, I cannot assist you in any way, dear friends and companions, I too am lost, broken, shattered, what shall I do?, the streetcar stops follow one another, outside there's an endless blotch of blurred faces, it comes to my attention that we're at the central station once I feel people pushing me from behind and toward the exit, I jump out of the vehicle, one can follow the same route for all eternity but one can never experience the same trip, well, that's not a novelty, is it?!, time varies accordingly to one's mood, could I, I would twist space, would now be aboard a ship, I walk among the crowd, someone bumps up against me and I nearly drop the newspaper on the floor, somehow I manage to keep it under my arm, hands still in pockets, I'm facing the streetcar central station, it would be nice to recover my hat before going to the bank.

I climb up the stairs leading to the main door, people come in and out, I pass by an undefined number of ticket booths, there are suitcases and bags scattered on the floor, on benches, wheelbarrows, thus present everywhere, some pieces of paper roll on the floor, I look for the lost and found office but cannot spot it, I inquire about its whereabouts, a conductor points down a corridor to my right, a most somber passage that I proceed to tread along, at its end I come across a desk with a sign reading "Complaints / Lost and Found," I walk a few steps forward in its direction, a clerk is resting her rotund breasts on the small counter, now there's a strange smell, not of sulfur or burning, a different odor penetrates my nostrils, it smells like vinegar and lemon, it's twisting and upsetting this delicate nose, my chest and back begin to ache again, it's a fragrance of paramount outlandishness, an unusual circumstance in this place, I reckon, clients should be respected, this acrid scent bothers me, affects my breathing capacity, I'm compelled to take a deep breath before opening my mouth to speak.

"Good morning."

"Good morning," answers the clerk, boredom visible on her face, another victim of apathy, she can barely move her lips.

"Yesterday morning I lost my hat on a streetcar. Aboard number 7, to be more precise, and . . ."

"A hat, you said? What does it look like, this hat of yours?"

"It's a short, crowned, black hat outfitted with a medium-sized brim."

"Wait a minute, please. I'll check if we have something in that style registered in our books."

The clerk trundles into darkness, the office is cluttered with objects, each with a numbered tag, daylight comes through two windows and falls on umbrellas, suitcases, hats, a bicycle wheel, wine demijohns, a birdcage, the clerk reads some sheets of paper with a pencil in her hand, which she uses to assist her in this intellectual enterprise, shakes her head a little, then returns to the counter, there's no one in line behind me, I can hear a buzz of distant voices, the wind seems to blow hard in this corridor, she shows me a paper.

"There's no entry regarding a hat found yesterday. Yesterday, only yesterday, sir! Of course, we have a fair share of hats in our office, but all of them were found earlier than yesterday. You can try to come back tomorrow or the day after, however, if no one has brought it here by then, you probably won't ever get it back."

"Yes, I see," and then silence ensues, perhaps I'm too feeble and about to collapse, lost my appetite and do not eat properly, thus I tend to forget that humans must eat, I miss some meals, when chewing I cause a stir with my chattering and noisy teeth. Now staring at the clerk and feeling dizzy, I nod. "Thank you for your time. Have a nice day."

"You too."

She rests her heavy breasts on the counter, the corridor casts shadows over her blank expression, turning my back on her, I'm suddenly attacked by the draft, at least it's not treacherous, the garlic woman on the streetcar didn't leave my hat at the lost and found office, or is the clerk toying with me?, one never knows, these people take a dislike to our faces, she might have seen the stains on my tie, deducing I'm poor—and it's true, I am!—a thug who can't afford to buy a hat, a mischievous fellow, oh, they act on the authority of a petty sense of morals, they let appearances deceive them, how many jobs did I lose because they don't consider me handsome?, yes, these people don't look beyond the surface, they're not human but monsters who suck faces, suits, hats, ties, skirts, trousers, walking sticks, in this oligarchy presumptuousness abounds, the conceited Szarowsky is one of its specimens, a behavioral model, a deadbeat who uses a grandmother's surname to show off his elegant breed, foreign names are more exquisite, the proof is well hidden in my pocket, I confirm its presence by touching it with a single finger, here's the check I will now collect, hopefully it won't bounce, refined people live amid great luxury but often don't pay their debts, they live on air and wind, such a lifestyle pleases our nation, and so they live the part down to the tiniest detail, if I entered the bank without a tie they would say

I'd stolen the check, whereas a man like Szarowsky, primly dressed from head to toe, owes money to half the world's population, I bet not even the suits he wears are paid for, the poor tailor must chew his nails out of hunger, nevertheless, when his excellency the lawyer asks him for another suit, he doesn't refuse, our people is easily bent, it's docile, kills itself without ever looking up, Helena went away and probably she'll be better in her new home, this land is condemned since the beginning of time, here dwells a people that neither rules itself nor lets itself be ruled, a people destined to travel, consisting of rats, they leap and jump on a dunghill, I'm surrounded by manure, what am I doing here?, there are grocers all over, lowlife merchants, swindlers, although they wear expensive garments, one can still imagine them using an apron, they pack a pound of rice with expansive solicitude, when I leave the station someone bumps against me once again, the newspaper falls from under my arm, no one hears my grumblings, I bend down to pick it up, my hands don't return to their respective pockets, I move ahead, a reluctant sun uncovers itself, my fingers quickly freeze in the cold wind, it's unpleasant, it smells of urine, the breeze brings me a whiff of human traces left near the buildings, not even rain cleanses them, some women sell fish on the sidewalk, they shout out loud and almost strike me deaf, this fish odor does not disguise the fragrance of urine, I close my mouth so as not to swallow the city's stench, our beloved metropolis is indeed a dunghill, those who live here for a long time end up rotting, we're alive on the outside though dead inside, absolutely putrid, it would be better if we all united and threw ourselves into the river, we would be washed out to sea, we'd lose ourselves in its depths, rid the world of such aberrations, we destroy everything, are parasites, Valido is a proglottid, a tapeworm, Szarowsky not even an amoeba, with some luck he could manage to be a bluebottle fly, and who am

I to utter these words of discontent?, I burn everything around me, can't make Helena happy, why keep on living if we cannot make our beloved ones happy, why do we work for these tapeworms if we can't be happy, we spill our blood in vain, so much effort just to hold off an inescapable death, man is the most pathetic being, an animal that doesn't see itself as an animal, but instead as a special entity, mankind raised above corporality and mingled with gods, now looks at the world it inhabits as if it were a demiurge observing his creation, man is aware of his death and thus suffers, however he can't deny with certainty that other beings share his sense of death, maybe they know they'll die but do not reflect upon death, only man is incapable of overcoming his end, truth be told, we're cowards, a destructive plague that would love to wreak havoc for all eternity, I walk up the bank's stairs, seagulls drawn by the fish for sale cry above me, this city is a true pigsty, it isn't easy to open the door, it's heavy, he who comes in enters a serious and respectful place, no doubt, it's hot in here, almost compelling me to unknot this suffocating tie, the cashiers are busy, I sit down and, opening the newspaper, wait my turn.

No news on ships, I sigh with relief, had already taken a look at the front-page news, life is a succession of tragedies, our people enjoy a good misfortune, we love to weep and lack a sense of subtle humor, a bunch of ignoramuses, now here we have an interesting article, in a small village a man came home and as he didn't like his dinner, he decided to beat his wife and children, nonetheless, apparently one kid wasn't in the mood for such a treat and began running around the table, he ran in circles and his father chased after him until another child, who previously had received his share of corporal punishment, tripped his father, who fell headfirst into the big pan over the fire, burned his head in an appalling fashion, they say all the village heard his terrifying screams, he was blinded, could still die, it took too long to get him to a hospital, the village doctor couldn't help him, now they don't know what to do with the kid who led his own father to this deplorable situation, some want to send him to a reform school, oh, that would be plain dumb, in our country no one thinks straight, the aforementioned kid should be rewarded, he rid us of another criminal, a genuine service to mankind and the world, he eradicated a public danger, our fatherland shelters no violence, here only good people prosper, life is good, the sun shines, we endure neither cold nor hunger, there's still an orange in my coat pocket, in fact I haven't eaten since yesterday's dinner, no, this land knows no famine, its inhabitants fast periodically and voluntarily, I do not eat because I don't wish to, my countrymen will no doubt do the same, please immediately assign this child to an important leadership role, finance his studies abroad, he can't rot in the countryside, he shows a more endeavoring spirit than me, I'm a slug, *kartofler*, goddamn, the word returns, I look up from the newspaper but the cashiers are still busy, the exact same people are standing in line, here business takes a long time, an urge to smoke arises within me for I am nervous, there's a faint smell of sulfur lingering in midair, I think about how I'm going to pay Valido a visit this afternoon, can't forget about calling on Madame Rasmussen either, maybe she can provide a feasible solution to my problems, although Hermengarda calls me an atheist, I prefer not to see myself as such, it's better to avoid all dogmas, my mind is open, completely stretched!, I won't say yes or no, perhaps I'm neutral in that field, a mere scoundrel, on the other hand, better to be neutral with gods than with humans, what matters did Teodorico and Hermengarda discuss with the critic?, that moron probably adores them by now, he'll heap praises on them as retribution for their kindness, he lusts for Hermengarda's body, sad fool, he'll never possess it, he'll return home to his wife, he's living on illusions, they all do, including me, the yellow house might be nothing more than an illusion, nonetheless while there's life, there's hope, that house is indeed a horse bit in my mouth, life pulls in the reins on me, I can't move my eyes, must always look ahead, when young they attached blinders to my bridle that I never managed to remove, here's another interesting piece of news, the city council is promoting a contest for the best original mask, an event to be held in their main hall, here's another one, a man dropped a wheelbarrow full of manure on the railroad and caused a derailment, an accident with no casualties, only some slightly wounded passengers, anyway there's manure strewn everywhere, sometimes I too can smell it, the cashiers take their time answering the clients' requests, it seems one client is taking his leave, he's going away, I close the newspaper, touch my breast pocket, take out the check, a cashier signals to me, wants me to approach, I stand up and walk, newspaper in one hand, check in the other.

"Good morning. I'd like to cash this check," and I put the check signed by Szarowsky on the counter, the cashier stares at me.

"Good morning. As you please, sir. Can you show me a valid identification document, please?"

"Of course."

I hand my parish registry card over to the cashier, he looks at me, confirms my identity, I straighten up, my posture is awful, ruins my back, he nods and gives me back the card, which I secure again in my trousers, the cashier rises from his chair.

"Wait just a moment, please."

He goes away, leaving me alone, at my side an old woman with a quivering head leans on the counter, presently she's counting the banknotes the cashier gave her, she looks distrustful, certainly didn't reach old age by letting any down-and-out sod swindle her, after counting and recounting the notes, she looks around and sticks them in a purse, which appears to be bigger than her, how can she carry that atrocity on the street?, the crone nearly bends herself in half, I straighten up yet again, will I reach her age, will we get old together, Helena and I, or will I die long before that?, will we be together, here or anywhere else, hopefully so, how can I live like this, I feel so sad walking the streets alone, don't know where to put my hands, how to move my arms, if I let them hang, or cross them over my chest, I look like an idiot who doesn't know what to do with his own body, the old woman puts a knit cap on her head, then looks me in the eye as if she would love to kill me, she's wearing mourning black, is the yellow house's owner a similar hag?, good gracious, and how old might Madame Rasmussen be?, I imagine her as a fat and decrepit lady, not so obese as Mrs. Lucrécia, but in any case even shorter, probably wears purple dresses, or lilac, or violet, her house may be stuffed to the brim with images of saints, holy men and women, and angels and crucifixes and flowers and akin objects, a devotional mishmash, does she live alone or not?, maybe she has a cat, the crone with the banknotes turns her face and moves away.

"Yes, go on, proceed with your life, hurry up," I say, and bang my fist on the counter.

A man must prove himself resolute when facing iniquity, the old woman doesn't look at me, perhaps she's deaf, a little demon, she exhaled a sulfurous fragrance, this city is full of minor demons, grotesque creatures that hide money in bags, drawers and mattresses, a sheer abomination, this city will burn out of rottenness, it's a dunghill they set on fire, the smell of burnt manure won't ever leave its inhabitants' bodies, it would be better if I forsook my intentions of buying the yellow house and departed for good, but where to?, I have no news from Helena, she will take a long time to send me a letter, an account of her new life, it's unbearable, I wish to leave and at the same time to stay, don't know what I desire, never did, lucky for those who know what they aspire to, we live an unhappy and aimless life, now and then I feel I could be happy nonetheless and deal with Valido, Szarowsky, Teodorico, Hermengarda, Mrs. Lucrécia, to have Helena here with me would be enough, on other occasions this world of mine sickens me, I wasn't born to live this life, I crave more, need money, why is it that everything I long for requires money, except what I want the most, although I need money to get it, money or a yellow house, isn't that so?, this is obscene!, my mind hasn't worked properly since I went to the pier, this disturbance has Helena's departure as its plausible origin, or conceivably a trip aboard an infamous streetcar, a vehicle from the depths of Hell, driven by a crook, the heads of garlic might be the ones to blame, they could be part of a scheme devised by that woman, not in order to ogle men's legs, but so one of them would touch the foul garlic and even leave a personal object behind, such as, for example, a hat!, yes, a hat she could use in all kind of wicked contrivances, though I've never believed in the black arts, I've always heard my parents and grandparents telling stories about toads with sewn mouths, dead chickens on crossroads, werewolves knocking at doors in the middle of the night, it's indeed a strange world the one we live in, ancient practices from a bygone era, and now?, science erased superstition from the earth's surface, not from mankind's heart, these atavisms condemn me to madness, I'm insane, I understand it now, I grab one thing while grabbing something else, I'm an atheist, agnostic, an unbeliever, I'm whatever people want me to be but, meanwhile, I'll visit a fortune teller, though it's absurd, there's no escaping, there's no causal relation in my actions, why am I standing here, in front of a counter?, oh, yes, I'm waiting for the cashier, he took my check, I'm lost, utterly lost . . . or maybe not, those around me seem to be in a worse condition, just watch the crone now leaving the bank!, the shrew eats money, lives only for it, is afraid of everything and everyone, I'm still quite rational, they intend to drive me mad but they'll fail, I'm indestructible, hunger compels me to contemplate disgusting possibilities, it's shameful, I'm sweating, my armpits are glued to my shirt, I try to calm down, it's too hot in here, I wish to take the orange out and eat it in order to refresh my throat, I'm dying, Helena is far away, on the high seas, she'll never know what happened to me, they will tell her I died, dropped dead on the bank floor, an apoplexy, perhaps a victim of the disease corroding my lungs from within, how my ribs hurt!, dear Heavens, the cashier is back, soon I'll be able to breathe fresh air again, the whispered voices torture me, I fell terribly sick.

"Thank you for waiting. Since the remitter has an account with our bank, I can cash it immediately. I will only need you to sign a few papers, sir."

"Of course."

The cashier's filling out all the paperwork, where's the blank spot I'll sign my name on, at last I'll get what's due, that thief didn't fare better this time, I laugh such a thunderous laugh, the open-mouthed cashier watches me, I'm invincible, everyone kneels in front of the great king, the emperor, I'm not crazy but am in fact this city's only reasonable citizen, the streets and houses have already burnt down, they're mere mirages, we inhabit a huge, steamy, ever-growing dunghill, we must remain on the surface or we'll be dragged to its bottom, whence it's impossible to escape, those who fall down the dunghill never stand up again, the flies that climb higher win, they try to throw me to the foot of the heap, not a single fly helps me, they could pull me up but instead they abandon me, I must fight to ascend, Helena is a flower at the top, sadly I can't see her, there's too much manure around me, everything's burning, burning!, castles in flames, the horizon is fading over the turrets, the walls are tumbling down, people scream, they're on fire, they're burning alive, I feel the ecstasy of the dying running through my veins, the doomed people's relief at their last breath, the sweetness of departing from life, it all ends in flames!, the smell is intoxicating, I cough and cough, surely blushing, the bank clients and cashiers look at me, while the world's burning they worry themselves with a man coughing in a bank's crestfallen silence.

"Are you alright, sir? Would you like a glass of water?"

"No, thank you, I feel fine, don't bother yourself with glasses of water," I say after catching my breath, the surprised cashier looks at me over a pair of glasses that slide down his nose, this cashier is reddish, his indoor life hasn't made him pale, maybe he owns some land where he spends his spare time planting vegetables, I'm sweating abundantly, and as the liquid spreads through pores and clothes, its smell prevails over the hellish fragrance permeating this city, the cashier offers me a few papers and does not know he's burning.

"You can sign here and . . . here, if you don't mind."

I sign the papers, my hand shakes mysteriously, a trembling caused by the shivers down my spine, were the money stolen I wouldn't be in a worse mood and less presentable, a degraded and degrading life wears me down, without Helena I perish in the eternal fire that consumes our world, fire whirlwinds feeding upon human flesh drag me, deafening screams and cries reverberate all around, the pen slips out of my hand, my name was signed with no zeal, twice!, probably a sign of faintness, I'd be wiser if I ate something, but then I'm not able to do it, food is irrelevant, an indestructible creature shouldn't need it, however, I'm a poor translator, not worth the air I breathe, treated like trash, they want to see me at the bottom of the dunghill, maybe they're right and I'm not respectable enough to make remarks on others, I suffer the same ailments, am a true son of my race, knowing no other perspective I center the world on me, see the world with my eyes only, if possible I would merge with Helena, would be her skin, spleen, a kidney, would be always with her and would neither commit mistakes nor make decisions, I will perhaps trip someone, burn their head, kill them, and finally be sentenced to the ship galleys, which I would gladly accept, want to be made a captive and sent to the colonies, scorch my brain there, die of fever after drinking filthy water, to be jailed can be a blessing, no decisions made as the time passes by, one can't fail, we're always the crystallized image of the last time we were seen, words written on letters fail less than spoken words, Helena said I'm crazy, life together was unbearable, the cashier stares at me, compares signatures, he doesn't seem particularly pleased, thinks I'm mad, can see it in his eyes, Helena was right regarding my intolerable presence, I'm a plague of fire, can't I end all this?, my God, the only thing left is to give her a small yellow house, yes, afterward I can be shredded into pieces, wouldn't mind it, the cashier takes back the papers.

"So, here you have the money."

He counts the notes, he puts them on the counter one by one, I confirm everything's right, tuck the money into my shirt pocket, assure myself it won't vanish into thin air.

"Thank you. Have a nice day."

"Have a nice day, sir."

I shake the cashier's hand, don't know if this is an accepted and civil behavior, I do it anyway, never knowing whether to greet another person I feel myself an outcast, ashamed of my gestures, this physical discomfort can lead me to shyness, I want to smoke a cigarette, have a pocket full of money, I leave the bank, it's much colder outside, an unpleasant wind blowing the clouds away makes me shiver and button up my coat while walking down the front steps, I throw the newspaper into the trash bin, don't want to read any more news, I'd rather not know anything, ignorance can be blissful, the streets are now quieter, people are working, my job, on the other hand, is flexible, it truly isn't a job for a respectable man, as Mrs. Lucrécia would say, she would love to see me working somewhere else, not at home, in order to let her save on candles and use the additional funds to stuff her paunch, she could keep more money under her pillow, I move away from the bank and toward a tobacco shop influenced by the desperate need to smoke, it's still early, I haven't eaten but am not hungry, I'll walk to Madame Rasmussen's office after buying some tobacco, we must take some illogical actions, there's nothing bad about it, I have enough spare time, the commercial letters can wait as I wait for my money, I don't care a fig, the world is burning and smells like manure and no one seems to notice such a phenomenon, at present I can only try to climb this dunghill to its top, where the air is purer, while I smoke another cigarette.

IX

I catch sight of the hardware store, its windows full of lockers, latches, nails, the sign plate has toppled and is only partly hanging, must be careful not to bump my head against it, a small boy runs to and fro on the sidewalk, he's probably the hardwareman's son, he enters the store, laughs at me when pushing the door open, it's a huge effort for such a little boy, feels he's a hero, doesn't know what's waiting for him, will spend all his life trying to recover his youth, not necessarily his infant years but those during which he had no worries, no checks to cash!, the most important thing in his life was his way of thinking, his ideas, he was the navel of the world, afterward he'll fall into oblivion, bloom, his petals will wane and the universe will forget and dismiss him, we all are nothing but a fleeting moment, a grain of wheat lost in a full barn, we survive through numbers, our quantity forces us to evolve and multiply until the end of time, nonetheless each grain must be ground so others can be brought into the barn, there's no turning back, we'll waste our whole life punishing ourselves for what we did and did not, a tragedy!, things could have been different, now there's no escaping reality and I'm facing the front door of Madame Rasmussen's building, can't walk away from here, her name is written on a little plaque under the doorbell, "Madame Rasmussen—Cartomancer, Fortune Teller & Paraphysicist," damn, this woman has an impressive background, I ring the bell, can hear how she opens the lock by pulling a string, the door opens with a snap, I step in.

Madame Rasmussen's apartment is on the second floor, I begin to climb the stairs, there's more light in here than in Mrs. Lucrécia's house, the stairs creak, all these buildings need repair, everything needs some mending, this city is sinking in mud, I quickly reach the second floor landing and see an open door, a woman thirty-five years of age awaits inside, she watches my movements closely, I stop and stand silent for a few seconds.

"Good morning, madam. I'm looking for Madame Rasmussen."

"Morning. I'm Madame Rasmussen. What brings you here?" answers the woman, pulling hair away from her face.

I'm surprised, I had imagined Madame Rasmussen as a much older woman, not as a woman in her prime, expected to find a rotting carcass dragging purple shawls behind her, a hag shrouded in flesh-squeezing waistbands, not this woman, how will I confide my problems to someone approximately my age, the smell of stew comes out of the door, it's not possible, unbelievable, these evil odors chase me far and wide.

"I would like to request your services regarding a most concerning . . ."

"Please come in."

Next thing I know I'm already inside the apartment, Madame Rasmussen has led me in and I didn't notice, this woman must have an incredible gift indeed, I was reluctant, hesitated once I caught a whiff of stew, she carried me anyway, it's a marvel, I feel less concerned about the smell now I'm in here, since it's her dwelling, it's quite natural that she's preparing lunch, she needs to eat as much as other people, spirits alone don't nourish her body, I'm the only one who survives with no food, has no appetite, am indestructible in my fasting, nothing can attack and prey upon me, now, it's an ordinary house, has enough furniture, no terrifying religious icons, I spot some books on the shelves, she appears to live by herself, a bright living room I had imagined darker, with tapestries and pieces of cloth blocking the sunlight, aiming to create an instantaneous impression upon the fools' senses, yes, I know she'll probably deceive me anyway, I can neither silence the skeptic in me nor bury myself deeper in this sordid matter, I bring a hand to my breast pocket, the wad of notes is still here, she can steal my money with her magical powers, or else with her conversational skills, how can one know, I'm a mere puppet!, someone else pulls the strings, am now sitting at a table in the living room, Madame Rasmussen closes the kitchen door and the smell of stew fades a bit, it's a relief.

"Please tell me what worries you and what led you to Madame Rasmussen and her superb services."

Referring to herself in the third person is not a good omen, however, after lifting a hand to my breast pocket I once again proceed with my explanation.

"My life is burdened with several problems. My bride moved abroad, I feel sick, some odors . . ."

"Be quiet! Not another word!" the woman yells so suddenly that I jump in the chair, when she speaks her brown hair falls over her face, she twists her fingers, the blue dress seems to darken as if by magic, yes, now we're on track, something will come of it, I'm sure. "You do not need to reveal anything more to Madame Rasmussen! Give me your hands."

This woman does not ask, she gives orders. Reaching out my trembling hands, I notice how badly my large nails need to be trimmed, my hands shake as at the bank, they do it out of cold or anguish or longing, Madame Rasmussen's face is hidden under her hair, oh, at this exact moment she's a sybil, a prophetess, I imagine her in ancient Delphos, the odors of stew are vapor rising from earth, my eyes I close, it's pleasant to have my hands thus extended, a warm and welcoming human contact, maybe I'm already cured, with eyes now open I ponder taking leave, I'm cured indeed, but she has other plans for me.

"You suffered a heartbreak! Yes, your bride left, I can feel it."

"Yes, I just told you . . ."

"Be quiet! Do not meddle with Madame Rasmussen's powers . . . I see a color . . . it's neither blue, nor green . . ."

"Is it yellow?"

"Yes, it is! Yellow, the color of something you most crave . . . it's not the sun but something more tangible."

"Yes . . ."

"A yellow house!"

"Yes."

Amazing, she truly has supernatural powers, she squeezes my hands, I notice she has green eyes, a probable means of attracting customers, Madame Rasmussen is a little rat, so am I, it's hot in here, I'm sweating, being close to a woman affects me, I yield to the basest atavisms.

"You work hard to get it . . . you're a clerk . . ."

"No, I'm not!"

"Your hands tell me you live among documents, papers, you're a man of letters . . ."

"Of course, they have no calluses."

"Be quiet! Are you mocking my supernatural powers?"

"No, not at all."

"Then show me some respect. If you don't believe, I can't help you. As I was saying, I can see you're a man of letters . . . a writer!"

"Well, not exactly."

"A reporter!"

I shake my head, would rather cut up this nonsense and go straight to the matter concerning me, I do not need a fortune teller to guess my profession.

"Listen, Madame Rasmussen . . ."

"Translator! You're a translator!" she says while rolling her green eyes in a fairly impressive performance.

"Yes, I am."

"And you wish to buy a yellow house for your bride, who moved abroad!"

"Yes, indeed. But, listen, I could have told you all that . . ."

"Be quiet, I command you! I've already told you to believe, you must believe, or it won't work. Want to know if you'll get the house and if your bride will like it, isn't that so?"

"Yes, that's quite it."

Madame Rasmussen rises abruptly, drops my hands, they land with a bang on the table, this is ridiculous, what am I doing here?, hunger clouds my mind, this smell of stew disgusts me, breathing some fresh air outside would be much better, she begins to chant an obscure hymn, I do not understand a single word she's singing and, all of a sudden, she knocks her head on the table, seems to have fainted, simply fell on the table and I don't know how to react.

"Madame Rasmussen?"

She's stands up, is flushed, sits down, smoothes her hair, she's bumped her forehead against the table, it's nearly lacerated, she seems dizzy, tries to speak.

"You will manage to buy the yellow house and your bride will return on a spring day."

"On a spring day? When? This year?"

"Madame Rasmussen does not know everything, only what she captures at destiny's crossroads. However, she sees the house will be yours to live in and you'll reunite with your bride."

"Well, alright, that's nice."

I cross my legs, Madame Rasmussen might not be a charlatan after all, maybe she's the recipient of an ancient kind of wisdom, science does not explain everything, some people have unknown powers, there's still hope.

"Madame Rasmussen, would you oblige me as much as to answer to one doubt of mine?"

"Of course, that's what I'm here for. Please tell me, you can entrust everything to Madame Rasmussen."

"You see, I'm haunted by strange visions and odors."

The fortune teller leans over the table, her forehead is still reddened, it looks swollen, it must hurt a lot, it's disturbing the way she stares at me, with that owl's expression, she wishes to impress me, draws her head near mine, goddamn, it's too much, I must get up from the table, my hands grip the back of the chair.

"Explain yourself in a more precise fashion: what type of visions and odors? Do they upset you?"

"Yes, of course they do. I'm afraid I'm going mad, last night I had strange nightmares, and despite knowing they're nothing but dreams, I can't stop feeling they're important, they have a veiled meaning. And I don't even know for sure if I slept or lay awake!"

"Please tell me more details."

I recount her my dreams, the nightmares in which Helena disappeared and I killed all the foes crossing my path, I fought continuously while distancing myself from her, the cartomancer listens to me, seems interested, her swollen forehead is appalling, it must be painful, she nods.

"Madame Rasmussen does know why you have those nightmares!" she says.

"Does she?"

"Yes. Those nightmares are a symbol of your fear of failing, of fighting in vain, of trying hard to join your bride and never succeeding. Mostly now that your bride went away."

Yes, of course, it's so simple, how didn't I think of it before, truth be told, I didn't think at all, I left home in a hurry, didn't ponder this matter, am going crazy, no doubt, I don't comply with the most basic rules of logic, need a fortune teller's assistance to understand what's filling my head, something which at heart I already knew, pathetic!, really grotesque, nevertheless, I'm still not satisfied and am at a loss to find an explanation for the smells, these hellish phenomena.

"And how about the smells?"

"What smells are you talking about?"

"Despicable odors of tar, sulfur, burning . . . for example, like the smell of something burning I'm smelling at this exact moment."

"The smell of something burning? Yes, it's true, it smells of burning!"

"Do you smell it too, Madame Rasmussen?"

"Of course!"

She gets up, walks, and then runs, suddenly opens the kitchen door and smoke invades the dining room, that smell of burning isn't surprising, the stew is combusting, Madame Rasmussen loses her composure, she swears and one can hear dishes carelessly thrown around, she's not a lady anymore, lacks finesse, curses like a drunk sailor in a bar, looks as if she forgot me, I wait and cough, smoke fills the room, this might be an evil sign, the fortune teller is a slave to the occult forces, I should leave, but first it's necessary to pay for this pleasant consultation, I do not wish more bad vibes on myself, she returns, the burning smell prickles our noses.

"Oh sir, a deplorable incident did take place."

"Maybe it would be better to come back another day."

"Yes, yes, of course, you must come back! We should solve several issues; the house will be yours, but you do need some help!"

Madame Rasmussen winks at me, I take the wad of notes out of my coat pocket, proffer a note that in my opinion seems quite a reasonable fee for such a service, she greedily grabs it, her eyes shine, forehead sparkles, good Heavens, what a swelling, if I don't leave soon this putrescent air will suffocate me, therefore I move toward the door, she follows me.

"Thank you. Farewell. And I wish you a swift recovery."

I point at her forehead, Madame Rasmussen touches it.

"Thank you. Do not forget to come back, you'll need several sessions to get the house you desire."

Thus having spoken, she closes the door in my face, the end is indeed less prodigious than the beginning, it's obscene, I'm a bit poorer and still upset, Madame Rasmussen has not solved my problems, honestly, saving me would be difficult, she burnt her stew, however, I won't give up, she assured me that house will be mine to own, yes, although I'm a man of reason, I've never expunged my superstitions, used to believe in Helena, she was my idol, now I have no idol to offer sacrifices to, I'll only get her back after buying the yellow house, it could be painted pink, it will be my greatest offer and my goddess will descend and keep me company, hence allowing me to worship her day and night, silently, for not to disturb this divinity, she's the only being rising above us, my daydream didn't mean a fear of failing, it was in fact a warning to renounce fighting, wallowing in mud, manure, until reaching the top, where Helena hovers with butterfly wings, that must be the explanation, my mind has still a few moments of clarity, despite the unwelcoming circumstances, I fight it with all my strength, and the house will be mine, I am going to work in order to achieve my goals and we'll never be apart again.

I climb down the stairs, go outside, the hardwareman's son is playing on the sidewalk, looks at me, smiles, I feel a great urge to contemplate the yellow house, the small boy waves goodbye to me and disappears into the store.

X

I'm ecstatic, can't wait to reach the little house, I decide to catch the streetcar, I walk to the stop, it's almost lunchtime and there aren't many people outside, a nearly empty streetcar arrives, the wind let up a bit and the sun's shining, truly auspicious weather in my opinion, I pay for the ticket, have enough money to pay for many tickets, must hide it well, touch it, a value still far from allowing me to buy a house, hopefully Valido won't take long to hire me, have to wait eons to receive my fees, weeks, months, years, with this series I can begin to save some money, shall get the deadlines and publication dates issue cleared, can't live on rumors, I sit down at the window, the streetcar heads off, I stick a hand out of the window and the wind freezes my fingers, I open my hand so as not to feel so much cold, a man stares at me from the other end of the vehicle, seems hypnotized, I wonder what he is thinking about me, well, that's neither there nor here, maybe we are just nothing in this world, I don't know if I dream or exist, the dunghill's in flames and a sea of mud and filth will swallow all of us, life is an abomination, don't know why I cling to it, the only explanation is Helena, everything desponds me, can't feel cheerful, Madame Rasmussen told me the house would be mine but I don't know if I should believe her or if I can believe her, skepticism always defeats me, I let hope die over and over again while keeping it alive at the same time, thought it sounds impossible that's what I do, don't ask me how, my stomach roars, warns me I must eat despite having no appetite, a nausea compels me to gulp whenever I think about food, the streetcar moves forward, I retract my hand, which is frozen cold, almost purple, my skin is dry, parched, I'm growing old, was young not long ago, years pass by and I have nothing to feel proud of, in my youth the possibilities were manifold, I could do everything and ended up being no one, yes, I'm a translator, I am what I do and am nobody, a name on a piece of paper, Helena departed, I wasted my life for years, postponed everything to get nowhere, now I must change, the time still at my disposal diminishes with each passing minute, waited too long, was a grown-up in my infancy and a child in my adulthood, I mixed everything up and ended up being only a middle term, an amor-phous substance, I'm facing its consequences, it's impossible to go back, I cheer up a little, the rails whine and sadden me, don't know exactly what's my current mood, wake up happy and lie down to sleep gloomy, on the other hand, when I wake up gloomy I rarely go to sleep happy, will the day come on which I will go to sleep sad and wake up sad?, what a wretched idiot, never knew where the wind was blowing to, nowadays I go with the flow, the streetcar stops, I've reached my destination.

Jumping to the sidewalk I immediately touch this dear breast pocket, touching important objects is an old habit of mine for fear of losing what's precious to me, it's quite a paradox, actually, taking into account that I lost Helena, though not completely, she departed, I stayed, we're still united, living together with me is unbearable but I don't give up, there's yet some sanity to be found in me, I feel ecstatic once again and smile, do not wish to stare at my reflection, which surely looks pathetic, I see the girl who was selling oranges yesterday, there's still one in my pocket but she smiles at me and I offer her a coin, then put the new orange in the other pocket, now my coat is well balanced, one orange at each side, I confidently approach the little yellow house, here it is, it's even more lovely in this bright light, I straighten my coat and the soiled tie, the crone is probably shortsighted, although I'm not sure she's old or has bad vision, my deductions regarding Madame Rasmussen were wrong, the cat is at the window, it's stretching its paws behind the window-pane to absorb the sun's warmth, I pull a rope, thus ringing a bell near the front door, hopefully the old woman is not deaf, I wait a minute, am too impatient, am nervous, ring the bell once more . . . ring it hard! . . . the cat's in the same spot, it's sitting idly, the door opens, I was not mistaken, it's indeed an old woman, I lean on the iron gate, she walks a few steps closer to some bushes, the cat jumps off the window, I smile.

"Good morning."

"Good morning."

"Do you own this house, madam?"

"Yes, I do. Can I help you?"

"Delighted to make your acquaintance, madam," and I proceed to present myself . . . to pull rank on her . . . I assure her I'm the most zealous worker, doing services to so-and-so, even getting to know, once, the queen . . . I'm an heir of an honest lineage, but also a busy man, so I continue. "Well, you may find this strange but, in short, I'd like to ask you to sell me your house. Would it be possible? Would you consider a serious offer?"

"Sell you my house?!" the crone seems confused, one can see the pinkish skin of her skull under her thin hair, and despite her fragile appearance, she's not hunchbacked. "You know, young man, I've never thought seriously about selling my little house, but some circumstances . . . please come in."

It's surprising, she invites me in, might it be a good sign?, the old woman drags herself to the gate, the cat peeks from behind the front door, I enter the small garden, she closes the gate, we stand face to face, she's a lot shorter than me, one can notice she's shrunk in her old age, her spine collapsed under the many years' weight, I must climb the dunghill before old age shrinks me and forces me to the bottom, I'm already past my prime, she smiles at me.

"You know something, young man, I don't usually open up for strangers. But I thought you had a nice, honest face!"

Of course, my job, the tie, the queen, all that improves my features, my aura, I certainly won't abuse or rob her, impossible!, I clear my throat, bow a little.

"Thank you, madam. My intentions are the best, I assure you. I apologize for disturbing you at this most inconvenient of hours, I am afraid you were preparing your lunch."

"Oh, don't worry, I've already lunched, I'm old and go to sleep very early, therefore I also wake up quite early . . . and my bladder . . ."

"Understood, understood! You're doing the right thing, living as we should, they say that waking up early is good for our health, it revivifies the body."

"Yes, I can't complain. Only about the bladder . . . a pity . . ."

Slow and suspicious, the cat draws closer.

"Well, don't want to waste your time, so let's talk business: yesterday my bride moved abroad . . ."

"You don't say! Did she move far away?"

"Yes, quite farther than I myself desired."

"For what reason, if I may ask?"

"She intends to start working at a new job. A friend called her, got her a new position over there."

"Hmm, I see, life's not been easy in our country. But will she come back?"

"I hope so. That's why I want to talk to you about this house. My bride adores it, and I would like to surprise her by buying it and turning it into our home. Does that make sense?"

The old woman smiles, perhaps my speech wasn't so ridiculous after all, she might be taking me seriously.

"I've lived here for more than fifty years and I'd never think about moving if I weren't so far from my daughter, she's the only family I have left, my daughter and no one else. She moved with her husband to another town and I've been thinking about moving too. Your visit is a happy coincidence, young man! You know, I'd never consider leaving this house if it weren't for that, no, never. Because of my daughter, I mean. I raised her in this house, and lived my whole life together here with my late Tomé, may God grant him eternal rest."

"I'm sorry for your loss, it must be devastating."

Devastating indeed, why didn't this nice old woman follow her beloved husband to the grave? Some marital bonds should never be broken.

"Don't feel sorry, that's how life works, and he did pass away many years ago!"

The cat rubs against our legs and then meows, I caress its shining fur.

"So, you might sell the house . . . for how much?"

"Oh, these vague ideas and possibilities . . . I've never pondered it so much as to reach a proper value, probably it would be better to talk with my daughter. But if you would be so kind as to pay me a visit in a near future, I'll be extremely pleased to discuss it further."

"Yes, I will surely call on you, madam."

"Do you want to take a look at the house?"

"If you don't mind."

The old woman smiles at me and walks toward the house, her gait's lighter than it looks, funny how old age transfigures a person, they either turn out to be more adorable or more despicable, this woman was lucky enough to develop her skills as a lovely old woman, I probably won't reach her age and, even if I did, I would never grow old with such graciousness, I'm rotting on the inside, am no more than a putrescent carcass, the cat follows her with a raised tail, I too walk and presently find myself in the hall, it doesn't smell of stew here, by Zeus, what a relief, the house itself is airy, though not very big, but the most important thing is that it doesn't smell of sulfur, burning, tar, or mud, one can breathe and we could live here.

"Come on in, please!"

"I don't want to disturb you, madam. I can take a good look at the house once I return in a few days, and then we can talk about practical details."

"Of course, young man."

The crone accompanies me to the gate, she's warming her bones, the cat follows her, it wants a treat, we shake hands and I make a gesture as if to lift my hat, damn, I keep forgetting I don't have a hat!, shameful, what she must think of me, she's not senile or blind, can see perfectly well how I'm presenting myself, nevertheless she said I have an honest face, not all is lost, she's interested in selling the house, maybe Madame Rasmussen was right, against all odds she might have supernatural powers, she's a true fortune teller, I must consult her again, but is it possible to buy the house?, Mrs. Lucrécia sucks my blood, the parasites don't pay me, is it really possible?, I look back and the old woman waves at me, the cat is at her feet, it curls around her legs, I hope she won't fall before selling me her house, falling at that age can be lethal, life's so transient, I'm being ridiculous, trite, longing affects me deeply, where might the ship be on which Helena is traveling?, I wonder what she is doing, this doubt occurs to me unconsciously, not even I realize that I ask no other question but that one, that's why I have nightmares, my life's a torment, my God, she departed only yesterday and I'm already in this miserable condition, a man quickly ruins himself, I'm completely crazy, it's a possibility, she was right when she ran away from me, left looking for a job she couldn't find here but also to escape me, oh, I burn everything around me, I too combust without noticing and drag down with me all those who try to get loose from the smoky dunghill, people come outside, they're hungry, there are two oranges and no appetite in my pockets, I'll walk to Valido's publishing house, its owner and manager is hidden in his den like a badger, the idiot eats breadcrumbs in order to save some petty cash, I'll walk in circles until the time of meeting is ripe, I easily forget to check what time it is, left my watch at home, on the desk, didn't wind it anyway, would trade it for a huge map, I check what time it is by looking at a church tower, I shrug, then begin my circular stroll.

XI

I'm determined to rush furiously into Valido's office, he only eats
leftovers and food scraps, rummages for rotting matter, a well-
defined lunchtime would be wasted on him, I feel slightly dizzy,
should eat but can't do it, am too anxious, my heart's beating as if
to jump out of my chest, my throat's throbbing, my ribs are hurting
anew, the fortune teller didn't mention any diseases, I'm surrounded
by charlatans, incompetents, there's no zeal for work whatsoever,
I shake my coat, don't know why, such as I don't know why I do
many things, a true mystery to myself, if I controlled all my gestures
and thoughts I would be a happy man, I knock at the door, wait a
little, the door opens up, I don't see a secretary, but two people I
know, Teodorico and Hermengarda, he immediately grabs hold of

my arm, the door is open, now I glimpse the secretary who assisted me yesterday.

"Hello, hello! Our dear friend the translator!"

"A real surprise!" Hermengarda laughs ridiculously like a schoolgirl, she does seem happy, as does her friend, I alone play the sullen part.

"Yes, a happy surprise, my friends. I wasn't expecting to see you here," and it is in fact a surprise, though a repulsive one.

"We had a nice little chat with Dr. Valido," says Teodorico, who apparently also knows in quite a detailed fashion the academic qualifications of the revered publisher. Next week Valido will possibly be a professor, since one invariably gets to a point in which such a promotion is inevitable.

"Oh, is it so? Any news?" I pretend to be interested when, truth be told, I am not.

"Yes," answers Hermengarda, "we will be published! Teodorico and I."

"You don't say! By Valido? Fascinating!" once again I'm not lying, it truly is fascinating seeing them both published by Valido, for he does not read unknown authors who don't have at least thirty years of experience in writing.

"And all thanks to our friend the critic! Yesterday, after you left, we talked to him and he recommended us to Dr. Valido, who was kind enough to call us to his office. We had our talent acknowledged by mere chance—how fortunate—and we couldn't have been happier," Teodorico squeezes my arm while he speaks, he's clearly exhilarated, Hermengarda laughs like an oaf.

"My congratulations, dearest friends. I'll be eagerly waiting for your books," and for the first time I'm not being honest.

"You'll get your own signed copy," Teodorico winks at me. "We won't waste any more of your time; we need to head to lunch, and you must work. We'll see you around, and don't forget to show up at the café so we can celebrate."

Teodorico shakes my hand, Hermengarda kisses me on the cheeks, they joyfully move away, the secretary is still holding the door open, her bangs seem longer, it might be an illusion, I once again smell an odor of sulfur when entering the office, she remembers me, guides me with theatrical gestures.

"I'll check if Dr. Valido can see you now. Just a moment, please."

"Thank you."

I'm disgusted at the recent news, thus are writers born, oh, I've never known which way the wind was blowing, no doubt, I lack the necessary cunning, my social skills only allow me to charm—momentarily—old women, such as my landlady or the yellow house's owner, maybe not even those two, Mrs. Lucrécia is pretty shaken from the incident that took place on the stairs, *kartofler*, damned word, it gets back into my thoughts, the old woman from the yellow house too might lose her illusions if I don't find the required money on time, I shall slam down onto her table a wad of notes, violently!, perhaps her daughter doesn't want her to sell the house, everything can go wrong, Madame Rasmussen might be right, but can also fail, I live under an uncertainty that shatters my nerves, can feel them breaking like glass, outside the sun is shining, while in this room darkness reigns supreme, the secretary returns.

"Dr. Valido grants you a moment of his time, sir."

Marvelous, what a great honor that of being able to stand in the presence of the weasel-king, a glorious occasion, now I can die in peace, she walks with me to his office, I feel like a stranger inside my own body, for a moment I do not know if I'm alive or simply dreaming, I might be a non-existent entity, Valido is sitting behind his desk, the weasel chews a bread crust, it's his lunch, I'd rather not eat at all than degrade myself like this illustrious publisher, the secretary leaves, closing the door, one can see perfectly how hard the bread is, a stale bread baked two weeks, or a month ago, there's mold on one of its extremities, all this is grotesque, there's not a single lit candle in the room, the sunbeams don't penetrate far into such a dungeon, the stinking badger eats with an open mouth, his intellectual looks suffer under such circumstances, he shows his true nature, he's a rat when eating, stretches his arm and invites me to sit down, I accommodate myself atop a pile of books.

"Good afternoon, my friend. I apologize for seeing you in my office under these poor conditions, but I was about to finish eating my lunch."

"Good afternoon. Don't worry, just proceed as you were. Maybe I called on you a bit too early."

"No, it's fine. My meal has dragged on a bit more than usual, for I've had a meeting with two young people we will publish soon, two new talented authors our publishing house has the pleasure to add to its catalogue. And young authors though they may be, they're highly recommended!"

Yes, once again the recommendations, the endorsements, the praise, nothing like having a good recommendation letter to move forward in life, sometimes even a few spoken words are enough, in this city references are more valuable than work skills, honesty, commitment, that's how things are, it's a valid system!, Valido resumes his speech after cleaning the corners of his mouth, they're dry, in fact he has nothing to clean, only eats crumbs, he muffles a belch and the smell of sulfur increases, I'm facing an abomination, a slave of the underworld.

"So, my friend, you've found yourself at our office. Tell me what brings you here, what worries you?"

"What worries me? Nothing, to be honest . . . Or maybe there's something worrying me, yes. You told me today we would discuss the details regarding my translation of the subsequent *Battle* series volumes, and that's my reason for disturbing you at such an inconvenient hour. Nevertheless, yesterday I heard some upsetting news. Probably rumors."

"And what do those rumors say?"

The weasel drags his fingertips over the desk and collects the bread crumbs, stares at me, doesn't notice I'm looking askance at the great publisher's miserable dessert, this situation is deplorable, in this dark little room one lives mankind's worst moments since we abandoned life in caves, his fingers touch his lips, yes, a consummated horror, the crumbs are digested.

"They say you wish to publish the series' second volume in two months. Besides it being, in my perspective, a rushed decision when the first tome has not been published yet, it appears to be a technically impossible feat, for one cannot translate so thick a book in such a short period. Unless you're not considering me for the job . . ."

Valido ruminates the crumbs, his scraps of food are an orgic meal, he suffers under the burden of so many expenses, war led to a rise in the price of paper, his income decreased abruptly, some tenants died in the trenches and he lost months of rent, the objects left in the cramped stuffy rooms were not sufficient to counterbalance his losses, oh, yes, let's take some pity on him, for he suffers atrociously.

"Right . . . Well, my dear friend, I wholly understand your concerns. We do, indeed, plan on publishing the book in two months, but the translation issue hasn't been decided yet."

"What do you mean? If you want this book to be out in two months, you must have decided on the translator. Even if it means having the book translated from a language other than the original."

"Certainly, but we're still considering our options."

"I don't understand: yesterday you told me I would have more time to do this translation than the time Szarowsky had given me. And you also told me you wanted me to translate the whole series. Is the situation different today?"

"Well, you see, we haven't decided yet! But, since you're here, would you care to comment on the changes made to your translation?"

"Changes? What changes?"

"The changes Dr. Szarowsky has made."

"The changes Dr. Szarowsky has made? What do you mean? I don't know of any changes. I never saw the book again once I delivered the translation two years ago!" Absolutely furious, I clench my fists. "I can't comment on what I don't know, but when I think that Mr. Szarowsky, who hadn't even read the book, wanted to change all occurrences of 'snow' to 'rain,' and replace all references to lakes with references to rivers because, according to him, the readers from this blessed country aren't familiar with such realities, what can I say?! Yes, what can I say?"

"I understand, but the changes . . ."

"Right, I see . . . oh, I see now what this is all about," I bang my fist on the desk, the sound reverberates on the wooden tabletop, Valido shrivels. "Just tell me please, out of curiosity: if you have already sent the book to print, and your daughter is painstakingly working on it right now to create yet another graphic gem, why did you summon me to your office and ask me to translate the series?"

That bastard, that weasel, that badger, that damned miser is taking away my bread and butter while he stuffs his mouth to the point he can no longer keep it all inside, spreading breadcrumbs all over his desk, over papers, over books!, he promises work and then he flees, hides away in his hole, changes, what changes?, these publishers and editors simply don't read!, for God's sake, this is intellectual indigence, the smell of sulfur thickens, it's unbearable, they disparage my work, Szarowsky's still causing me harm, the imbecile, another weasel, a deadbeat, he has always questioned my work, he couldn't stand me, what did I do to him?, nothing!, if only he got run over by a streetcar, left to rot in a bloody mush, what a fine day that would be, what a fantastic day!, the weasel doesn't give me a direct answer, he doesn't know what to say, doesn't have to, he's asked someone else to do the translation and doesn't want to admit it, they're all cowards, in this city nobody ever takes responsibility for their actions, some of them promise things and then suddenly disappear without giving any explanations, nobody keeps their word, they're piles of manure, they're the ones who create the burning dunghill, piece by piece, excrement over excrement, a living treaty on scatology! . . . this is intolerable, what am I expecting to hear from Valido when he has nothing to say to me?, his actions are not based on logic, what drives him, him and all the others, is interest, collusion, betrayal, incompetence, Helena has left all this behind, she made the right decision, one can't breathe here, the ass is quiet, his jaw moves in perpetual rumination.

"Well, I see you have nothing to say to me and I refuse to have my work questioned by Szarowsky, a crook, a man who doesn't even know what a lake is and who doesn't understand a single word of the original language. The insolence of his revisions! He can't even speak our language! Pretentious fool! Did you know that that presumptuous fool's last name isn't even Szarowsky?"

I bang my fist on the desk again and get up, the weasel seems to have sunk some more into his chair, he's a dry withered fig, the room is filled by sulfurous vapors, I turn to the door, but presently I take the oranges out of my pockets.

"Here, you need this more than I do! Cherish them dearly, now you have enough food for a whole week!"

I toss the oranges onto the desk, then I pick one up and feel the urge to throw it at him, however, I only make the gesture, Valido's eyes flinch shut and he doesn't say a word, his expression of fear makes me want to beat the hell out of him, he's despicable, revolting, I'm not going to ruin my life over a spineless worm, I peel the orange I'm holding in my hand, toss the peel on the floor and break the fruit apart, put a piece in my mouth, chew it and feel the juice on my tongue, place the rest of the orange on the desk, next to the other, I walk to the door, open it, I prepare to leave.

"Just one more thing, Mr. Valido: *kartofler*!"

The old man startles, he jumps in his chair, he didn't see this one coming, a slap to the face, *kartofler*, *kartofler*, *kartofler*, can't remember what it means, shall have to look it up but I have so much to do, I leave Valido and the oranges behind and hastily cross the office without greeting the secretary, I refuse to speak with servants of Beelzebub, slam the door when I leave, I feel a sense of relief, will never be summoned here again, will never be offered work by them, I couldn't care less, they've stabbed me in the back, they're worms, there's nothing for me to do here, I'm not wasting any more time, I'm going home, there might still be some leftovers from Mrs. Lucrécia's lunch for me, I'm not hungry but need to eat, the most important thing is the yellow house, I won't make any money here, there are no translation jobs available, but who cares?, it would take ages for me to receive everything they owe me anyway, there has got to be another solution, nothing's lost, the sun is shining and Madame Rasmussen assured me the house would be mine, I cough, I'm having a fit of bronchitis, something's affecting my lungs, they want to destroy me but I won't let them, I'm going home, back to Mrs. Lucrécia's stews, that miser, she keeps her money under a pillow, yes, I wonder how much money she has, probably a fortune!, yes, that's it, maybe I can ask Mrs. Lucrécia for a loan, no, she's too stingy, she would never lend me the money, what if, well . . . why don't I just take some money from her? . . . relieve her from its burden . . . the old hag's starting to get a stiff neck, she's growing a hump for sleeping on such a large stack of notes, this situation requires my full attention, I need to make sure that what the maid said is true and act rationally, can't lose focus, must maintain my critical reasoning, a coherent thought, it's not easy when everything around me is burning, the world is succumbing to flames, it smells of burnt tar, I hear screaming voices, it's horrible, where is Helena now?, do they offer oranges on the ship?, I miss her so much, if I were that kind of man I would cry, my chest hurts, can't breathe, I pull myself together, people were beginning to stare at me, the madman!, I decide to take the streetcar back home, any thoughts I might have about moral questions slowly fade away with the movement of the vehicle along the rails, I'm just a translator, not the champion of human justice, they're pulling me down, I'm swimming in sludge.

XII

Time runs fast, the streetcar trip is like a void, I don't know how I got in and out, today's driver could have been the scoundrel I know, the driver of the streetcar that made my whole life go off the rails . . . what am I saying, my life was already in shambles, it has been for years, I'm ludicrous, an atheist who pays for visits to fortune tellers, so much for logic, I'm not the only one though, everyone finds themselves doing things and making decisions they can't explain, surrendering to foreign actions and gestures . . . mimicking the absurd . . . they're overcome by bizarre humors, maybe it's our body's way of making us wake up and face reality, we're all burning in the same dunghill but nobody can see it, why do we need eyes if we can't see a thing?, damn, it's a natural aberration, the wind is picking up again, it's getting chilly, I see some clouds drawing near, I almost trip on a child running past me, he's carrying a sack of coal on his back, he smudges my pants, I don't care, can't be bothered to clean them, all of this is sordid, I haven't thought of a way to get into Mrs. Lucrécia's bedroom yet, she never leaves the house, I walk a few more yards, I see a group of people near our building, the door is wide open, the maid is outside, she's pale from having spent her life among pots and pans, there's a woman complaining in the hall, I don't recognize her, Miss Sancha is also there when, in fact, she should be working, I don't see the student, something's definitely amiss, I can't spot the landlady, I finally arrive.

"What happened?"

"You have no idea," the maid says. "Poor Mrs. Lucrécia's a wreck!"

"A wreck? What do you mean?"

"She fell down the stairs," the maid replies. "We found her sprawled out and unconscious on the floor!"

Miss Sancha is crying, she dabs at her eyes with a handkerchief and nods to me, she's corroborating the story, the unidentified woman folds her arms, she's approximately my age and has a sulky expression, the maid carries on, this will probably be the most exciting day in her whole dismal life.

"Mind you, she fell while going to your room."

"To my room?"

"Yes, by lunch time Mrs. Lucrécia wanted to check if you were feeling well, since you hadn't come down for breakfast . . . this is terrible!" says Miss Sancha.

That damned stingy, prying old hag! She had to go upstairs just to spy on me, she's always sticking her nose in other people's lives, I bet she climbed the stairs up and down in the dark just to save on candles, that meddling miser, the maid isn't satisfied yet, she loves the attention she's getting with all this commotion, some passersby stop to see what's going on, some linger for a while longer.

"They had to take her on the fruit wagon, poor thing."

"Oh my! On the fruit wagon!"

"Yes, I'm telling you the truth, nothing but the truth . . . We sent for Mrs. Lucrécia's niece right away. She's the next of kin, you know . . . See, I remembered that Mrs. Lucrécia has a little address book, so I looked for it, and here she is."

So, the sulky-faced unidentified woman is the old fart's niece, the hag has a family, after all, unbelievable, she glances at me and offers me her hand with disdain, I repay with a cold grip of her fingers.

"Are you Mrs. Lucrécia's niece?"

"Yes, I am."

"Pleased to meet you," I greet her.

"Pleased to meet you too," she replies. "Such a dreadful accident. I assume you're the tenant who rents the first room . . ."

"Yes, I am," I reply, Miss Sancha cries. "How is your aunt?"

"We don't know yet, but it's serious, very serious. I will obviously move here and look after the tenants while my aunt recovers. I will occupy my aunt's room today, and I can assure you that major changes will be made to the way this house is run. We don't want anyone else falling down the stairs."

"Certainly, certainly!"

"This house has been very poorly run. And this obsession with saving on candles . . . it's a health hazard."

I was right, Mrs. Lucrécia could have been more cautious and taken some candles with her, but she didn't, so now I've got her niece right in front of me, the grotesque creature stares unpleasantly at me, her hairy eyebrows seem to be pointing right at me, might she be implying I'm the reason why the house has been badly run?, and today of all days, after having seen my work threatened by two condescending snobs, this is all a great indecency, an outrageous disgrace of biblical proportions, a deluge wouldn't be enough to clean so much trash, but I'm not throwing in the towel, never!, I will not take the blame and keep quiet.

"Indeed . . . the lighting . . ."

"Yes, we'll talk about that later. And I'm afraid you'll have to dine elsewhere, if you don't mind."

"But of course, given the events . . . The shock . . . And to be carried on the fruit wagon!"

"I know!" the flustered maid yells.

The women talk, I can't hear what they're saying, the new hag is now going to occupy the bedroom, I might as well forget about the money—if there is any money at all!—no, won't be able to do it with this hag there, the first thing she'll do will be to check the drawers and under the mattress, she's expecting this to take long, she's not even making us dinner, it's obscene, the old hag's still breathing and her niece is feeding off her warm flesh, just another parasite, I really do live on a dunghill in flames, no question about that, even a blind person can see it, what shall I do now, where will I get the money to buy the house?, will the old woman sell it?, I'll never be able to afford a house by the looks of it . . . literary translation jobs paid years and years after they were due, the odd commercial letter, abject poverty, this is all a man's life amounts to, and then one day we end up on a fruit wagon!, could I work as a streetcar driver?, but with my feeble lungs and the drafts inside the streetcar, it could be dangerous, very unsafe health-wise, what shall I do?, by Zeus, what a miserable life, Helena, where are you?, is the weather sunny there on the open sea?, here the clouds are piling up, it's going to rain, I left my umbrella on the coat hanger but don't want to go back there, the women are talking, they can't seem to keep their mouths shut for a second, I move away from them soundlessly, they don't realize I'm gone, I turn back, disappear round the corner, still hearing the howling that is going on in front of the building, walk down the back street, a dirty alley, really, and catch sight of our squalid yard, I clamber up the small wall, and advance through the vegetable garden, I use a wood log for support and peek through Mrs. Lucrécia's window, her room is empty, the door is half open, her pillow is on the floor, the bedding completely scrambled, I try to unlock the window to no avail, I almost slip but hold on to the windowsill and smack my face against the glass, I scrutinize the bedroom interior, Mrs. Lucrécia's niece looks through the door, her mouth is wide open, we exchange glances, I hastily step down from the log and start to run, I clamber back over the small wall and run down street after street, I am mortified!, don't know what I was thinking when I did that, after all I've got some money in my pocket, I do!, what good is money anyway, I miss Helena, what on earth am I doing here without her, climbing windows with the help of logs, I fall and fall, I keep wallowing but I remain in the exact same spot, I walk without standing, she's far away and I'm not moving, I run through the streets as if I was being chased by the police, some people stare at me in astonishment, I'm not sure where I'm running to, I cross squares, avenues, boulevards, nothing can stop me, not even hunger, everybody wants to destroy me, I will never set foot on a streetcar again, don't stop running, I run to where I saw her for the last time, my movements are controlled by grief as I head for the harbor.

XIII

The world is a dunghill in flames, all this water before my eyes couldn't put out the fire, we shall burn till the end of our days, I want to burn with Helena, there's nothing else for me but her, she has only left yesterday but I'm devastated, won't be able to cope if I go on like this, I must buy the house as soon as possible, but how?, my legs ache, I've got this annoying cough, I'm no good, have no skills and a feeble body, there are no other options for me, I'll have to carry on making a living as a translator, I must gulp and carry on, I'll never buy that house, Helena is probably laughing right now on the ship, she's leaving misery behind, I burn everything around me, I'm not sure whether it's actually the world that is in flames or if it's just me, because I'm the only one who can smell these smells, the sulfur, the tar, the everlasting burning, am I the only one who can see reality or the only one who's burning?, I will never know either if we all feel the same, or what I actually feel, there's a hole in my chest and another one in my head, the worms have taken over my body, I kill my foes, yet I can't seem to reach her, she runs while I stand still, she's on a ship exactly like these, people smile and wave while they climb aboard, farther down the road the streetcar rings its bell, I'm drenched in sweat, my stomach roars, I'm walking to and fro on a small fishing pier, rotted wood boards squeak under my feet, I'm perfectly aware that I am talking to myself, loud and clear, the seamen cast suspicious glances at me, they think I'm drunk, they laugh out loud, pointing fingers, I feel flustered, overcome by madness, don't know what I'm doing here, I look at the water, turn back, run to the streetcar stop and sit on the bench waiting for nothing, feel once again a constant pang in my chest, how can a translator live without his bride?, I have no idea, storm clouds darken the sky, it's going to rain, I cover my face with my hands, haven't shaved in a long time, my skin feels rough, I cough, was startled by my own reflection in the water, people stare at me, disgusted, I have reached my lowest point, am fighting against myself and defeat is certain, Madame Rasmussen hasn't helped me, it was a mistake, a streetcar stops, I don't notice who gets in and who gets out, I bury my face in my hands, hear the rails screeching from the torture inflicted upon them by a sadistic driver, my stomach is eating itself, for a brief moment I feel well, hunger helps clear my mind, it's a relief really, I feel a persistent touch, a finger is tapping my back, I lift my head.

"I'm so glad I've found you! I have your hat. I've carried it with me ever since you left it on the seat."

The voice I hear belongs to the woman from the streetcar, the one who dropped the heads of garlic, her radish nose now resembles a potato, yes, that's it!, *kartofler*, that's what it means!, everything makes sense now!, perfect!, lovely!, she's got my hat, I feel my shirt pocket and the banknotes inside, I've got everything sorted out, I'm going to travel, be close to Helena, that's the solution, we don't need to delve too much into things, in the end everything works out for the best, the woman smiles and extends her arm to me, holding the hat with her fingers, I take it, put it on my head, let it sit on my skull.

"Thank you, ma'am, much appreciated."

She smiles.

"First, I thought about leaving it at the central station, but then I said to myself how lovely it would be to see you again and give the hat back to you in person."

She smiles, I do the same, at least I think I'm smiling, I stand up, she is shorter than me and still smiling, her eyes gleam.

"I can't thank you enough, ma'am."

"I would be very pleased if you'd walk me home. And I would feel rewarded."

I notice that old smell of burning, a sulfurous steam exudes from her mouth, a mighty gauntlet stirs the dung, the world is shaken by the Creator's claw, making men stagger, they try to stand, the wind drags the screams away, ah!, we're all consumed by flames, a man should never turn back, what a shame, indeed, how sad, however, decisions have been made, the wind blows undisturbed, everything works out for the best.

"I'm terribly sorry to disappoint you, but I won't be able to do that. I'm otherwise engaged."

The woman looks down, her smile fades, I take my hat off and place it on her head, I glance at the river, the sun's rays have pierced through the clouds and the water mirrors them.

"I don't need the hat. I would like you to keep it."

"But . . ."

"Do you know what *kartofler* are, ma'am?"

"Pardon? I don't think I understand you."

"Who understands me, anyway? Only my bride!"

I walk away, leaving behind the garlic lady, she's standing at the streetcar stop wearing my hat, only it's not my hat anymore, I'm going on a trip, Helena is somewhere on the blue patch on the map, I look back one last time and start running, I cross the rotted wood pier, the boards moan under my weight, the seamen are watching me, I don't stop running, I run even faster, reach the end of the pier, jump into the water, the blue dark green gray water, I hear a woman's scream and men shouting words into the wind, the current is strong, I can't smell anything here, the water is so calm, cold, and peaceful, so quiet, the world ceases to burn, there's enough water to put out the flames, the current takes me along, I let myself go with the flow for a while, I swim farther, someone throws a lifebuoy at me, it falls short, some fishermen push off a small boat, I refuse to hold on to the lifebuoy, it's humiliating, a piece of driftwood passes by me, it's too lightweight and too small to keep me afloat, a crowd gathers on the pier, the fishermen draw near me, I attempt one last arm stroke, why can't people just leave me alone?, I want to float, to move my legs, I will reunite with her, I'm a translator, I have unfinished jobs laying on my desk, someone will finish them, none of that matters now, Helena, my bride, is waiting for me on the pink patch on the map and, to meet her, I must swim across that entire length of the deep ocean blue.

João Reis, born in 1985, is a Portuguese writer and a literary translator of Scandinavian languages (Swedish, Danish, Norwegian, and Icelandic). He studied philosophy and has lived in Portugal, Norway, Sweden, and the UK, having worked in several different occupations, from book publisher to kitchen chef. Though still an emerging author, Reis's work has already been compared to that of Hamsun and Kafka, and represents a literary style unseen in contemporary Portuguese writing.

**OPEN
LETTER**